Praise for Greg Sarris

How a Mountain Was Made

How a Mountain Was Made

Stories

Greg Sarris

HEYDAY, BERKELEY, CALIFORNIA

Library of Congress Cataloging-in-Publication Data
Names: Sarris, Greg, author.
Title: How a mountain was made : stories / Greg Sarris.
Description: Berkeley, California : Heyday, [2017] | "These stories first
    appeared in the Federated Indians of Graton Rancheria's tribal newsletter."
Identifiers: LCCN 2017007459| ISBN 9781597144148 (hardcover : alk. paper) |
    ISBN 9781597144230 (e-pub)
Subjects: LCSH: Miwok Indians--Folklore. | Pomo Indians--Folklore. | Coyote
    (Legendary character) | Folklore--California, Northern. | Indians of North
    America--California, Northern--Folklore
Classification: LCC E99.M69 S37 2017 | DDC 398.209794--dc23
LC record available at https://lccn.loc.gov/2017007459

Paperback ISBN: 978-1-59714-473-5

Book Design: Ashley Ingram

Published by Heyday
P.O. Box 9145, Berkeley, CA 94709
(510) 549-3564
heydaybooks.com

Printed on demand by Lightning Source, USA

10 9 8 7 6 5 4 3 2

In gratitude to the mountain

Contents

Part 1

*T*his is the story of Sonoma Mountain. It isn't one story; it is many stories that make up the one story. The stories go on and on because the Mountain itself has so many things— rocks and animals, birds and grasses, fish, frogs, springs and creek, trees—and each thing has a story. Many of the stories connect with other stories. This makes sense, because the animals and plants and all other things on Sonoma Mountain connect with one another.

The Mountain has always been a special place for Coast Miwok people. The stories from the Mountain teach important lessons, and many of the songs that Coast Miwok people have sung since the beginning of time are gifts from the Mountain and come from the stories. It is said that Coyote was sitting atop Sonoma Mountain when he decided to create the world and people—but that is part of the big story of the Mountain and we are getting ahead of ourselves.

The best way to hear the stories is to listen to Coyote's twin granddaughters, Answer Woman and Question Woman. Some people say they are a pair of crows that sit on a fence rail partway up the Mountain, near the place folks call Gravity Hill. Other people swear Answer Woman and Question Woman are humans; these people claim to have seen the twins, two identical-looking women with long dark hair, leaning against the same fence rail, talking. In any event, Answer Woman and Question Woman have been on Sonoma Mountain a long time—they are the granddaughters of Coyote, after all. They know all the stories. But this is their predicament: Answer Woman knows all the answers but she cannot think of them unless she is asked; Question Woman, on the other hand, cannot remember a single answer, not one story, and she must always ask her questions in order to hear the answer again.

Yesterday I stopped and listened to them talking.

Question Woman asked Answer Woman about the smooth round rocks in Copeland Creek. "Sister," Answer Woman said, "you never remember a thing, so I will tell you about those smooth round rocks again."

And that was when I overheard the following story.

The Pretty Woman and the Necklace

*T*here once was a very pretty woman who lived near the top of the Mountain in a village alongside the headwaters of Copeland Creek. She fancied a young man from the bottom of the Mountain who lived in a village at the edge of Cotati Plain. The pretty young woman's father was a well-respected man; he possessed many songs, and people near and far sought him for advice and to hear his songs.

"Father," the young woman said to him, "there is a man I fancy at the bottom of the Mountain, and I worry that he will not find me attractive."

The father couldn't believe his ears. "But how is that, Daughter? You are young and beautiful and come from good people."

"Ah, but Father, this young man lives at the bottom of the Mountain, in a village at the edge of Cotati Plain, and many people pass through that village. He must see many beautiful young women every day. I must stand out; I want him to see me and no others."

The wise father advised her that she must not push her luck, that she should stand before the young man on her own merits. He reminded her that pushing one's luck, much like trickery, often brought about regret. Then he made a beautiful necklace of abalone pendants and clamshell disc beads and gave it to her. "Wear this necklace when you visit the young man," he advised her. He showed her how to double the beautiful necklace around her neck so that the young man—indeed all of the people in the young man's village—would know who she was and where she came from.

But the pretty young woman wasn't satisfied with the necklace. She didn't think the beautiful necklace was enough to attract the young man so that he wouldn't take his eyes off of her. That night she dreamed of a hillside—she actually knew of the hill, which wasn't too far from her village—and she saw a string of rocks just below the hill's crest. "How beautiful those rocks looked," she said to herself when she woke up. "Those rocks looked like a magnificent necklace on that hill." She figured if she couldn't stop thinking about those rocks then neither would the young man she fancied.

But how would she make a necklace from those rocks for herself? Then she got an idea. She would ask the animals for help. After all, she did have special songs from her wise father for the purpose of talking to the animals. Bear could carry the rocks; but Bear was forgetful and might lose his way to the hillside. She would have to ask Cooper's Hawk to hover over the spot so Bear could look up from time to time and know where to go. Then, once the rocks were piled at the creek, the dirt and lichen would have to be cleaned off of them. She would ask Fly to do that. And then, before the rocks were made smooth in the water, they would have to be ground down to size. She would ask Pileated Woodpecker to grind down the rocks.

So she sang her animal songs, and first she spoke with Cooper's Hawk. She said, "Cooper's Hawk, you fly so high; no one can miss your outstretched wings. Will you do me a favor?"

Cooper's Hawk, perched on a bay laurel branch, agreed to help the pretty young woman and asked what she wanted.

"Will you hover over yonder hillside where a string of rocks stretches below the crest of the hill?"

With the pretty woman's request, Cooper's Hawk flew off, singing this song:

> *Where I am looking,*
>
> *Where I am looking,*
>
> *Even the smallest mouse I can see*

Then the pretty young woman spoke to Bear. "Bear, you are so strong; you can run up the Mountain as if it were nothing. Will you do me a favor?"

Bear, sitting upright alongside the creek, agreed to help the pretty young woman and asked what she wanted.

"Will you go to yonder hillside where Cooper's Hawk flies and carry back to this place many of the rocks that stretch below the crest of the hill?"

Then Bear ran off, singing this song:

> *Light as a feather,*
>
> *Light as a feather,*

Straight ahead I go

Next the pretty young woman spoke to Fly. "Fly, you work so hard; you can work all day at the most tedious job without getting tired. Will you do me a favor?"

Fly, sitting on a stone near the gurgling water, agreed to help the pretty young woman and asked what she wanted.

"Will you clean the dirt and lichen off of the many rocks that Bear will pile here next to the creek?"

When Bear left the first rock, Fly got busy and was singing this song:

Small as I am,

Small as I am,

Even the rustling wind doesn't forget me

Finally, the pretty young woman spoke to Pileated Woodpecker. "Pileated Woodpecker, what a wondrous beak you have; you can drill holes in the hardest wood. Will you do me a favor?"

Pileated Woodpecker, clinging to the side of an oak tree, agreed to help the pretty young woman and asked what she wanted.

"Bear has carried many rocks to the creek from yonder hillside where Cooper's Hawk flies. Fly is busy cleaning the dirt and lichen off of them. Will you use your powerful beak to grind the rocks down to size so that I can make a necklace with them?"

"Sure, but how many rocks do you need ground down to size?" asked Pileated Woodpecker.

"I'll tell you when there are enough," answered the pretty young woman.

Pileated Woodpecker shrugged his shoulders and then went to work chipping the rocks down to size. All the while he sang this song:

No headache,

No headache,

But dreaming of nuts

But the truth is the pretty young woman didn't know how many rocks she needed for the necklace she wanted. Soon it was winter. Cooper's Hawk was still flying above the hillside. Bear had carried many rocks by then. Fly had cleaned many of the rocks and kept the cleaned ones in a separate pile. Pileated Woodpecker kept chipping away and had by this time many round rocks of various sizes, though hardly enough rocks the right size for a necklace.

"Keep working," the pretty woman said to the animals.

Then it began to rain. At first the pretty woman wasn't concerned, but before long she could see there was a major storm upon the Mountain. The headwaters of Copeland Creek swelled and spread, so strong that the torrential waters began carrying the rocks downstream. "Never mind, keep working," the pretty young woman said to the animals.

It rained and rained. Soon nearly all of the rocks went crashing down Copeland Creek. "Never mind, keep working," the pretty young woman said again and again.

Cooper's Hawk was the first to speak then. "I quit. I'm not going to hover over yonder hillside any longer. If I keep flying there and Bear takes all of the rocks, where will I hunt for mice?"

Then Bear spoke up. "I quit too. If Cooper's Hawk doesn't hover over yonder hillside, I might forget where the rocks are and keep traveling until I am lost."

Then Fly spoke. "Getting lost would be the least of your problems, Bear. You need salmon for that strong body of yours. Without salmon you will die. The wind tells me when the salmon are coming up the creek, and if I am so busy cleaning dirt and lichen off of these rocks, then when will I have time to listen to the wind? So, I must quit this business too."

Finally, Pileated Woodpecker spoke. "Me too. I must quit. If something happens to Bear, then who will I have to knock acorns out of the trees for me each fall? Who else is that tall and strong?"

"Oh, please keep working," the pretty young woman pleaded. "What else am I going to do? I must have that necklace!"

A large ripple of water rose up then and took the last of the rocks.

"Tell me, what am I going to do now?" the pretty young woman hollered.

The animals could see that the pretty woman was extremely upset. And she was mad at them for not helping her any longer. They thought of suggesting she go to her wise father and ask his advice. But they knew she would not go to her father. Besides, the animals knew that her father would tell her that she had pushed her luck instead of standing on her own merits. Her father had given her a beautiful necklace, which was all she needed to attract the young man she fancied at the bottom of the Mountain. She was tricked instead by her insecurity and a silly dream.

Yet, even if the animals wanted to speak again with the pretty young woman, they could not, for she had run down the mountainside chasing after her rocks. Copeland Creek emptied those rocks near the bottom of the hill, just past the bridge on Lichau Road. When the water is low, during the summer, you can see the round rocks of various sizes scattered about the creek bed. And summer nights, when the moon is full, the rocks look like large eggs. Sometimes you will see the pretty woman, not so young anymore, wandering about, wondering how she will get someone to help her make a necklace.

Part 2

*O*ne morning while visiting at their usual spot near Gravity Hill, Question Woman commented to her twin sister, Answer Woman, that the two of them never argued. "We get along so well," said Question Woman. "Why is that?"

Answer Woman said, "We need each other. Look, I know all the answers about this Mountain, but I cannot think of them unless you ask me. You cannot remember a single answer, not one story, so you must ask the questions in order to hear the answers again. Together we can hear the stories and know the important lessons they have to teach us about Sonoma Mountain. If you and I argued with one another, if we didn't talk, we would get nowhere up on this wondrous Mountain."

"But Crow and Buzzard argue all the time," said Question Woman. "Just yesterday, where Lichau Road crosses the bridge, I saw the two of them quarreling terribly. Crow was squawking on a fence post. Buzzard was humpf-humpfing on the ground and looking up with an angry red face at Crow. Tell me, why do they fight?"

"Ah, clearly you forgot the story," said Answer Woman. "Come, let us sit together in the warm sunshine, and I will tell you the story of our father and our uncle."

Crow and Buzzard Have a Hunting Competition

*C*row and Buzzard were brothers. Crow was the younger brother, swift and smart; Buzzard was the older brother, strong and hardworking. They lived in that village at the headwaters of Copeland Creek. Coyote was their father, and Coyote was the chief of the village at that time—which was when all the animals were still people. And Crow was a young man at that time, not yet Old Man Crow.

Crow and Buzzard often hunted together. Crow, being swift and smart, could chase rabbits and deer through the brush, and he knew how to herd them directly to his brother. Buzzard, so strong and hardworking, would wait behind the trunk of a giant old oak tree and then catch the animals with his enormous bare hands. Together, the two brothers were successful hunters; they brought plenty of meat back to the village. Of course they each had powerful hunting songs. And they knew never to take from the Mountain any more than they needed.

One day they decided to have a contest. It was the middle of winter and the people of the village were hungry. "Go and bring back meat for the village," Coyote told them. "My sons, you are fine hunters."

No one knows which of the two brothers came up with the idea for a contest, whether it was Crow or Buzzard who first thought of it. They still argue, blame each other. At the time, each of them thought it was a good idea. They figured if they competed with one another then they would be able to bring meat back to the village sooner because they would be working harder and faster. But Crow had his own reason for wanting a contest. Quail was the most beautiful maiden in the village, and Crow wanted to impress her with his success. And Buzzard too had his own reason for wanting a contest. He had heard some people in the village say that he wasn't very smart, and he wanted to show them that he was just as smart as anyone else and didn't need his brother to help him hunt.

So off they went in separate directions. Crow followed the Mountain's ridge north, toward Santa Rosa. He was singing his hunting song:

> *Better to run*
>
> *You know I am looking*
>
> *Better to hide*
>
> *You know I am coming*
>
> *Hey-hey hey-hey*

There is a valley below the mountaintop, just west of the village, and that was where Buzzard went. Buzzard was singing his hunting song:

> *The old oak tree is your house*
>
> *This way, this way*

No rain, no wind in your house

This way, this way

Hey-hey hey-hey

So each of the brothers went along singing. Crow discovered many rabbits and deer running, and he chased after them. But to his dismay they did not stop. They kept running. For four days and four nights the rabbits and deer kept running and Crow kept chasing them. Back and forth they went, north then south again, along the Mountain's ridge, first the rabbits and deer and then Crow chasing after them.

Crow figured at some point the rabbits and deer would get tired. Still, they kept a good distance ahead of Crow. And Crow could not hear them singing. The rabbits sung thus:

Oh, the bulbs are waiting

Oh, the wild carrots too

Oh, the blue dick bulbs are waiting

Oh, the wild carrots too

It is winter, after all

And the deer sung thus:

Keep to the Mountain's top

We see the ocean yonder west

Keep to the Mountain's top

Fog and clouds yonder west see us

Buzzard, meanwhile, was hunting in the valley below the mountaintop. He wasn't having any luck either. The only big oak trees there were at the edges of the valley. The rabbits and deer in the valley would not go near the big oak trees because they knew Mountain Lion waited to catch them there. So Buzzard, sitting behind a big tree, sang and sang his hunting song but to no avail. The rabbits and deer, keeping away from the big oak trees at the edges of the valley, couldn't hear his hunting song. "I'm so hungry now, I'll eat anything," Buzzard said.

Then, on the fifth day, a fierce storm broke over the Mountain—wind and rain such that people had never seen before, and thunder and lightning. Some people say Crow lost his senses and became confused, while other people will tell you that Crow actually wasn't all that smart to begin with. But this is what happened: Crow was tired from chasing the rabbits and deer back and forth, north then south again, along the Mountain's ridge. And now he was wet and cold too. He saw the leaves of a bay laurel tree glinting from the rain. The sun was breaking through the clouds. Crow thought he had found a tree of beautiful shining abalone pendants. Well, he thought, if I can't catch rabbits and deer for that beautiful maiden Quail, then I shall impress her with these beautiful abalone pendants.

Buzzard, meanwhile, looked up to the Mountain from his lowly place behind an oak tree and saw the rabbits and deer relaxing in the emerging sunshine. What happened to my brother, Buzzard wondered. Where did Crow go? Certainly he hasn't caught any rabbits and deer. Neither one of us has caught any rabbits and deer.

And that was when Buzzard all at once grew red in the face. He wasn't so stupid, after all. He realized that he had been prideful and greedy. He wanted to show off, and to do that he had planned to take more from the Mountain than he needed. He had allowed himself to be tricked, thinking that he could hunt alone, without Crow, his brother.

"Younger brother, it is your fault, it is your fault, it was your idea," Buzzard said as he began to climb the Mountain. But just then a big wind came to chase away the last of the storm; and because Buzzard was so light from not eating, the wind lifted him into the air, and that is where he remains with his embarrassed red face today. And the only way he can hunt is by the smell of rotten flesh carried in the wind. Which is why he is stuck eating only rotting animals.

And Crow, who hadn't yet understood how he had been tricked by his pride and greed, walked back to the village believing Quail would instantly fall in love with him when she saw the abalone pendants. When he opened his hand to show her the pendants, she immediately started laughing at him, for what he was presenting her was a handful of wet bay laurel leaves.

"Those bay laurel leaves can keep fleas away," she said. "Do you think I am full of fleas?"

Then the whole village was laughing.

"We needed meat, not bay leaves," said Coyote. He pointed to Buzzard flying helplessly over the village with his red face. "What fools I have for sons."

Crow found he could not hunt without his brother Buzzard. His hunting song was useless. Which is why today he is a scavenger, eating leftovers, or whatever he can steal from others. And he is still fooled by shiny objects, picking them up and carrying them back to where he lives.

"It's your fault," he says to his older brother flying on the wind with a red face. "It was your idea."

Then, sometimes Buzzard will come to ground, and the two of them argue back and forth about whose idea it was to have a competition and hunt alone. But, of course, in all that arguing they still miss the point that they must work together.

Part 3

*O*ne day Question Woman was curious, which of course was not unusual, given that curiosity was her usual state of mind. She was sitting with her twin sister, Answer Woman, in their usual spot next to the fence on Gravity Hill. Below them spread all of Santa Rosa Valley, and on this clear summer afternoon they could see as far as the ocean, all the way to Marshall and Tomales Bay.

"Tell me, Answer Woman," she asked, "how do stories come to you?"

"Quite simple," answered Answer Woman. "You ask me a question and my answer comes up in the form of a story. After all, the best answer to anything will always be a story."

"But I still don't understand. Where are the stories located? Where is their home?

"Stories are like invisible seeds," answered Answer Woman. "They live in the very air we breathe. They are around us at all times. When you ask me a question, it is like one of the seeds has been watered and a flower grows, one of the everlasting spirits, and it talks to me. That is my power, my gift—to understand what that invisible flower spirit is telling me. But, of course, the flower spirit is not awakened, the seed doesn't sprout and grow, without your question."

A cool breeze blew up the Mountain and both sisters

looked west. In the distance, they could see the fog hovering over the western hills. They saw big, puffy white clouds ready to march across Santa Rosa Valley and up Sonoma Mountain.

"Why does the fog come up the Mountain here?" asked Question Woman.

"Oh, that is quite a story," answered Answer Woman. "The story is speaking itself to me now. Here is what it is saying."

Mole Finds

Two Wives

$\mathcal{F}$licker had no husband. Yet she had a son, Mole, who was a very handsome young man. They didn't live in the large village near the headwaters of Copeland Creek but in a smaller village on the eastern side of the Mountain. Not many people lived in this village, but of those who did live there many were old men.

"Which one of you is my father?" Mole would ask the old men.

"I am," answered Yellow Jacket.

"I am," answered Flea.

"I am," answered Blue Jay.

"I am," answered Bear.

So the young man was frustrated. His mother wouldn't provide him the kind of answer he wanted either.

"Who is my father?" he asked.

"They all are," she answered. "After all, each of the old men in the village has looked after you and cares about you."

Some people said Coyote was the father of the young man; others said it was the Sun. No one knew for certain, and Flicker never let on. Instead, she told anyone who asked just what she told the young man himself: "My son is fortunate to have so many fathers, all of whom are old and wise and care about him very much."

Sometimes the old wise men gave Flicker advice.

Yellow Jacket said, "Be gentle so the young man will grow up kind."

Flea said, "Stay close to him so he will grow up comfortable and not be fearful."

Blue Jay said, "Sing to him so he will always know where you are and learn the value of songs."

And Bear said, "Teach your son to work so he will grow up strong and not be lazy."

She took the advice of the old men and raised her son well. Sometimes she spoiled him, however. Nothing terrible, for she kept to the advice of the wise old men, and Mole grew up to be a good and hardworking man. But she liked to keep him happy at mealtimes. Sometimes, particularly during those long winter months when there wasn't much else to eat, she saw that he grew tired of eating acorn mush. Then she would find dried salmon and dried berries for him. In the spring, she saw that he grew tired of eating clover and miner's lettuce. Then she found seeds that she had stored away and made him warm pinole. "What's the harm in pleasing him this way?" Flicker said to herself. "My son is a good and hardworking man."

Then it came time for Mole to find a wife. "Now, more than ever, you need the advice of your many fathers, the wise old men," Flicker told him. "I cannot ask for you. You must go yourself and ask." Which was what Mole did.

"If you want a good wife, be kind," Yellow Jacket told him.

"If you want a good wife, be warm, stay close to her," Flea told him.

"If you want a good wife, be talkative, let her know when you are home," Blue Jay told him.

And Bear said, "Son, you must be hardworking if you want a good wife."

"Thank you, fathers, that is good advice," Mole said. "But tell me, how do I get a good wife?"

At that point, Hummingbird came walking along. Hummingbird said to Mole, "Son, have you forgotten that I am your father also?"

"I should have known, another old man who is my father," Mole said. "Maybe you can tell me how I can get a good wife."

Hummingbird laughed out loud. "I hope you are not asking for pity—or even for special songs. You are a fine-looking young man and you are good and hardworking. You can have your pick of women."

"But how do I know if a woman is good?"

"You must follow your heart," answered Hummingbird. "And one more thing: Each good woman has a song and you must learn to hear that song and answer it with a special song that she will teach you, for only that way will you be her true husband."

"All right then, thank you for the good advice," Mole said.

And with the good advice of his fathers Mole went off looking for a good wife. First, he went to the large village near the headwaters of Copeland Creek. He found no women there who spoke to his heart. Then he went down the Mountain to the village at the edge of Santa Rosa Valley. No women spoke to his heart there either. He went further, to Petaluma, and found no available good women. Finally, there he was on the western slopes above Tomales Bay when he spied a beautiful woman walking up the hill from the water. She wore a dress of glinting abalone shells, and on her head a white cap made from goose down. And she was singing a beautiful song:

> *I am coming*
>
> *Singing, I am coming*
>
> *The people of your village rejoice*

Mole was enchanted. "Who are you?" he asked.

"I am Fog," she answered.

His heart told him he had found a very, very good woman. She was lovely to behold and her song was the most beautiful he had heard.

"If you would so honor me, would you teach me a special song in order that I might answer your song and be your true husband?"

"Ah, you have been advised well," Fog said to Mole, and she sang thus:

> *Standing on Sonoma Mountain*
>
> *Looking west*
>
> *I wait for you*

I am here

Standing on Sonoma Mountain

Looking west

Each and every summer

Waiting for you

And that way, singing, he led her across the valley and up Sonoma Mountain to his village. Upon seeing Mole's wife, the villagers rejoiced, just as her song foretold. Everyone was pleased. And, as it turned out, she became a good friend to all. "Thank you for advising my husband well," she told the wise old men. "Thank you for raising such a fine man," she told Mole's mother, Flicker. She was an excellent wife. She and Mole had many children. "My goodness," Flicker said, "Fog, you are even a better mother than I was."

Fog, in her kindness and wisdom, replied, "Flicker, with children equally good, how can one compare parents?"

Then one late winter day, while Mole was hunting on the far eastern side of the Mountain, he came upon another beautiful woman. She was standing on the edge of a meadow full of sun. She was quite tall, her head reaching the branches of the pine trees there. She was singing thus:

Coming from the east

Hailing from the great valley

I'm coming

And the people of your village rejoice

The song was beautiful, and Mole was enchanted.

"Who are you?" he asked.

"I am called Warm Wind," the tall pretty woman answered.

Mole's heart told him he had found a very, very good woman. She was lovely to behold and her song was the most beautiful he had heard.

"I have already found a good wife. Why have you come?" he asked her.

"I come through this meadow on my way to the ocean each year at this time. You haven't noticed me before?"

"Well, I already have one wife and that is enough," Mole said.

Warm Wind said nothing. Mole was about to turn around when a thought occurred to him: I can sing many special songs and be a true husband to any number of wives. As long as I sing my special song each and every summer to Fog, she will be content. If I learn to answer Warm Wind's song with a special song, I can have her for a wife also. When Mole looked back to Warm Wind, he saw that behind her, where she had walked, the meadow was full of flowers: poppies, lupines, lilies, blue dicks, a host of beautiful colors as far as he could see. He thought to himself, Yes, winter has been cold and long. I want this good woman. Where she walks it is spring. So he said to her, "If you would so honor me, would you teach me a special song in order that I might answer your song and be your true husband?"

"Ah, you have been advised well," Warm Wind said to Mole, and she sang thus:

> *At the meadow's edge*
>
> *Looking east*
>
> *I wait for you*
>
> *I am here*
>
> *Standing at the meadow's edge*
>
> *Looking east*
>
> *Each and every spring*
>
> *Waiting for you*

And that way, singing, Mole became Warm Wind's true husband. But Mole did not take her back to his village. The meadow was warm and he liked it there. He built a house for Warm Wind and together they had many children. As it turned out, Warm Wind was an excellent wife and mother.

Then one day, when it was very hot, Mole wished for cold weather and rain. Oh, now if only I could meet a good woman who could bring me those things, he thought. And, lo and behold, there across the pond, where he had been cooling himself with water, stood a beautiful woman. She wore a full-length cape made of white eagle feathers. She sang thus:

Coming from the north

Ice and rain

I'm coming

The people of your village build fires

But even before Mole heard the last line of this pretty woman's song, he had seen that all around her the earth was dry and the leaves of the oaks were turning colors and falling to the ground. Thus he realized summer had passed and he had forgotten his first wife, Fog.

He raced back to his village, but alas Fog was nowhere to be found.

"You forgot our mother," his children cried, "and you forgot us."

He ran then to the edge of the Mountain and began singing Fog's special song, but to no avail. She appeared along the tops of the western hills but would come no closer.

Then he ran back to find Warm Wind. To his surprise, he found her in the village.

"Don't bother coming back to the house at the edge of the meadow," she told him. "My children and I are ashamed of you. What do any of us want with a man who cannot remember his wife and children? Go hide yourself, shameful man."

Which is what Mole did. He went off and dug a hole and has lived there in that hole ever since. He sings thus:

Blind, I am looking

In my shame

I live

Warm Wind went back to her house. Still, each year at the end of winter, she walks in this direction. And Fog, the big puffy white clouds you see on the western hills, she comes up this way every summer, never forgetting her children and all her friends from Mole's village. Sometimes, lonesome for the children and her friends, she can't wait for summer and visits at other times too.

Part 4

*I*t was another warm spring day. Lupines and poppies blanketed the hillsides of Sonoma Mountain. Clover blossomed in the meadows. Question Woman and Answer Woman were in their usual place next to the fence on Gravity Hill. They could see west clear to the ocean and east clear to the top of the Mountain. There was a comfortable breeze, and Question Woman and Answer Woman could see the leafy branches of trees gently bobbing. There were bay laurel trees and oak trees, pine trees and buckeye trees too, and all of them looked as if they were waving to the twin sisters seated there below the fence.

"It must be hard being a tree," said Question Woman. "Trees are stuck in one place. If a breeze comes along, they can stand and wave. Otherwise, they can do nothing." Question Woman then pointed to the flowers on the hillside. "The flowers too, they cannot get up and walk around but must stay put all day."

"Ah, dear Sister," responded Answer Woman, "you are saying the trees and flowers have a difficult, less fortunate time on this earth than those of us who can move about. That is not so. In fact, in many ways, those of us who walk about or fly in the air are not as lucky as the trees and flowers. Certainly, we are not any more special."

"Why is it things aren't always what they seem?" asked Question Woman.

"That is why we have stories—to remind us that the world isn't always how we may be thinking about it," answered Answer Woman. "The stories remind us that the simplest of us might be the most complex and that the smallest of us are powerful and important too. For example, it certainly isn't a bad thing to stand in one place all day. The trees and flowers, in fact, live quite well. Let me tell you the story."

Centipede Calls

for a

Footrace

*T*his happened at the big village near the headwaters of Copeland Creek. At that time, many people lived in the village, and they were happy. There was plenty of food and the people had time to make beautiful baskets and shell ornaments. People from far and near went up Sonoma Mountain to trade with these villagers. Nowhere else could people find such beautiful objects.

Centipede lived there with his wife Bumblebee. Centipede was known as a fine athlete. He could go great distances without getting tired. He walked all the way to the Russian River and found the place where the best blackberries grew. Then he packed many baskets of large blackberries back to the village. He walked all the way to Stewarts Point and found the place where the best oak trees grew. Then he packed many baskets of large acorns from those trees back to the village. He worked hard and was greatly admired amongst his fellow villagers.

One day in the middle of winter it was raining and Centipede had nothing to do. Bumblebee was busy cooking and taking care of their daughter, Potato Bug. Potato Bug was a large girl and liked to eat, and she kept Bumblebee busy all the time. Other people in the village were busy making abalone shell necklaces and beautiful beaded skirts and colorful headdresses. These beautiful objects and those who made them were greatly admired. Besides the gifted people who made these beautiful ornaments, there were men and women in the village who made good houses, and of course these craftspeople were greatly appreciated also.

"Oh, have you seen the headdresses made of golden flowers?" Bumblebee asked. "The neighbor girl who makes the headdresses is such a smart young person."

Centipede wanted to make his wife and daughter happy. He went to the neighbor girl who made the headdresses of golden flowers. "Smart young girl," he said to her, "can I trade you a cache of good acorns for two of your headdresses?"

"Oh, Centipede," she said. "You have brought me acorns all year long. You may have two of my headdresses without trading anything."

Centipede thanked the girl and then gave his wife and daughter each a beautiful headdress. Bumblebee was happy, but as soon as she put on the headdress she returned to her cooking. Potato Bug was happy too, but as soon as she put on her headdress she returned to her bowl of acorn mush.

All right, thought Centipede, to get my wife and daughter's attention, I will ask the expert hut maker to build a beautiful house. With a beautiful house, I will not only get my wife and daughter's attention but also keep it, for everywhere they look while they are in the house they will be reminded of what I did for them. Then he went to the expert hut maker. "Smart old woman," he said to the expert hut maker, "can I trade you a cache of good acorns for a beautiful house?"

"Oh, Centipede," she said. "You have brought me acorns all year long. I will build you a beautiful house without trading anything."

Centipede thanked the old woman and in no time she built a beautiful house for Centipede and his family. Bumblebee was happy and so was Potato Bug. But before long, Bumblebee went back to her fire to cook more food and Potato Bug went back to her bowl of acorn mush.

Centipede was distraught now. He felt his wife and daughter didn't pay him enough attention. And the people of the village, busy making baskets and necklaces, didn't give him enough attention either.

Now that it is winter, what can I do so that my wife and daughter and all of the people of the village will admire me the way they do in the summer and fall when I go far distances for blackberries and acorns? wondered Centipede. Somehow I must have all of the beautiful objects so that people will notice and admire me now in winter. I must surround myself with abalone necklaces and pendants; I must have a storehouse of fine headdresses and beautiful skirts; and I must have several good houses.

That was when he got an idea.

He called together his friends and told them to meet him at the far edge of the long meadow east of the village.

To Bluebird he said, "My friend, you are rather plain looking. Wouldn't you like a bright blue cape?"

To Squirrel he said, "My friend, you are certainly plain

looking. Wouldn't you like a silvery coat?"

To Robin he said, "Look at you, my good friend, you are so dull in appearance. Wouldn't you like an orange skirt?"

And to Cricket he said, "Wouldn't you like a green vest the color of spring grass? Look at how uninteresting you appear without such a vest."

"Well, how do we get such things?" they all asked Centipede.

"We will have a footrace," Centipede told them. "Bluebird, you will race the woman who makes the bright blue capes and, when she loses the race, she will have to give you a cape. Squirrel, you will race the woman who makes silvery coats, and Robin, you will race the woman who makes orange skirts. Cricket, you will race the woman who makes green vests the color of spring."

"But these women are very fast runners," protested Centipede's friends.

"Ah, but you must take a chance. How else are you going to get the beautiful clothes that you want? I will challenge my young neighbor who makes the headdresses of golden flowers, and you know that she is one of the fastest persons around. I am a fine athlete and very strong. However, I am slow. And, still, I am not afraid to challenge my neighbor to a footrace."

"Well, if you're not afraid, we must not be afraid either," they said.

Centipede's friends went back to the village and made

their challenges. Centipede challenged his young neighbor, and she said to him, "Okay, but if I win the footrace against you, what do I get?"

"You will get a large basket full of the best acorns," he told her. "If you lose, you must give me four of your headdresses."

So on a day it didn't rain, Centipede and his friends met again at the far edge of the long meadow east of the village. First, the woman who made the bright blue capes came along. Bluebird raced this woman across the meadow, but, alas, Bluebird lost the race. Then the woman who made the silvery coats came along. Squirrel raced this woman, but, alas, Squirrel lost the race. Next came the woman who made orange skirts. Robin stepped up to race this woman. But, alas, the woman who made orange skirts pulled ahead of Robin and never looked back. Then the woman who made green vests the color of spring showed up, and it was Cricket's turn to race. Cricket was speedy, but not speedy enough to beat the woman who made green vests.

"This was not a good idea," Bluebird said to Centipede. "What were you thinking?"

"Ah, don't worry," answered Centipede. "You have lost nothing. I was the one who paid each of your challengers a large basket full of the best acorns. And, look, you've been sitting around all winter and now you've had some exercise. Quit complaining."

At long last, Centipede's neighbor came along, the talented young woman who made the headdresses of golden flowers.

This young woman was especially fast, faster than any of the women who had raced against Centipede's friends. Knowing how slow Centipede was, she figured she would win the race easily enough, though she never said anything to Centipede so as not to hurt his feelings. But, as it turned out, this young woman found that even before she and Centipede were halfway along the length of the meadow, she grew tired and couldn't maintain her fast pace any longer. Centipede won the race and got four beautiful headdresses from her.

"Something must be wrong," this young woman said. "I must race you again and try to win."

"Well, that's fine," said Centipede. "Let's race again."

But again the young woman grew tired and lost her race against Centipede. Four times she raced Centipede and four times she lost. Centipede now had won sixteen headdresses made of golden flowers. The young woman who made the golden-flowered headdresses was so exhausted that she lay down in the meadow and fell fast asleep.

Then Centipede sent his friends back to the village to tell the expert hut maker that he wanted to race her. Remember, the expert hut maker was an old woman, but she was very swift.

When the old woman arrived at the far edge of the meadow, Centipede said to her, "If you win the race, I will give you a large basket full of the best acorns. If you lose, you must make me four of your beautiful houses."

The old woman agreed and figured she would win the race

easily since Centipede was so slow. She took the lead and was far ahead. Centipede was just going along in his slow way. That was when his young neighbor heard him singing thus:

With the power of a hundred legs

I move

With the strength of a hundred legs

I am moving past you

Hey-hey hey-hey

He thought the young woman who made headdresses of golden flowers was fast asleep, and he kept singing this song as he passed her. Immediately the young woman knew something was terribly wrong. She jumped up and began shouting to the swift old hut maker. "Stop! Get out of here. Centipede is singing a song and casting a spell on you. I heard him singing!"

Then everything made sense to Centipede's four friends. They understood how they had been used by Centipede to help fool everyone into believing that if they lost their races then surely Centipede would lose his.

"Stop the race!" the young woman continued to shout. She was excited now and frightened. "Centipede has tricked us and he means to get all of the beautiful things we make. It is a trick. He is casting a spell."

And with that, all of them ran back to the village. They ran as fast as they could, leaving Centipede alone in the meadow. In the village they told everyone what Centipede had done. Everyone grew frightened, especially the craftspeople who made all of the village's lovely objects and beautiful houses.

"Soon he will reach the village and then he will do something to get all of the headdresses," said the young woman who made the headdresses of golden flowers.

"He will take all of our beautiful houses," said the old woman hut maker.

"He will take everyone's abalone pendants and necklaces," said the necklace maker.

"He will take all the beaded skirts," said the skirt maker.

These people, who made beautiful objects, ran off in every direction. Some went north, others went south. They ran over the hills. As far as people could see, the makers of beautiful objects were running. At last, night fell, and they could see no longer where these people had gone.

When Centipede reached the village, he found the people extremely angry. Coyote, the headman, stepped forward and said, "Look around, Centipede. All of the people who make beautiful baskets and necklaces have fled the village because of what you have done. You were greedy. You wanted more than your share and sought to trick people to impress your wife and daughter. Now our village will not have the wonderful necklaces and headdresses that brought us so much good attention. Not only that, we will have no one to make us good houses and we will have to go through winter wet and cold."

Which was what happened. The houses were flimsy and didn't keep the people dry and warm during the winter. And people from other villages didn't go up the Mountain to trade with the villagers at the headwaters of Copeland Creek.

Then one day toward the end of winter, Bluebird was walking along the mountaintop. Like the other neighbors, he was very sad. He felt particularly ashamed because he had taken part in Centipede's plan to get all the great and beautiful objects. He missed all of the people who made these great and beautiful objects. He sat down on a rock and began to cry. "I miss you," he said out loud. "I miss you. I am sorry for what I did with Centipede. Please have mercy."

When Bluebird got back to the village, everyone began to gather around him for they had seen what he had not yet discovered—he was wearing a bright blue cape. Bluebird ran back to the place where he had sat on a rock. All around him were beautiful blue irises, the first flowers of spring.

"Is it really you?" Bluebird asked. "Are you the woman who once made bright blue capes?"

Then he heard a song:

> *Look at me and don't forget*
>
> *My name is Iris*
>
> *Blue, Blue, Blue, Blue*
>
> *I am the first flower of spring*

And then Bluebird looked and saw that the entire mountainside was dotted with wild iris. He promised Iris he would never forget her, then ran back to his village and told everyone what had happened. Next Squirrel went out and found the woman who made silvery coats. She was now a wild onion blossom and she too was scattered all over the Mountain. She gave Squirrel a silvery coat, and he promised always to remember her. Robin went out next and found the woman who made orange skirts, and she was now a tiny forest orchid. Robin apologized profusely for his part in Centipede's plan and he promised never to forget her. Then she gave to Robin an orange skirt. Finally, Cricket, walking about, called to the woman who made the green vests the color of spring grass. "I am sorry. I am sorry," Cricket said. "Have mercy on me." And below his feet he saw a bunch of showy clover, and this showy clover gave him a green vest the color of spring.

Before long all the people of the village were out calling for all the talented people who had left. "We are sorry," cried the people of the village. "We miss you." And one by one the great people who made beautiful objects and houses revealed themselves as plants and trees and taught the people once again how to make beautiful baskets and good houses. The woman who once made beautiful baskets was now sedge, and she taught the women who found her to make baskets with her roots. The expert hut maker was now a willow tree and she taught the men and women who found her to use her strong branches for the foundation of huts. On and on it went, until the people of the village found everyone they had lost.

From that time on, the villagers paid tribute to the plants and trees. Each spring the villagers called out the names of the plants and trees. The Mountain was beautiful with all those plants and trees, and the people had food and shelter because of them. That is why the Coast Miwok people give a Spring Ceremony. Each village leader gets on top of the Roundhouse and names every plant and tree. If any one tree or plant is forgotten, it is said that the plant or tree will forget the people. It will leave the people and may not be found again for a long time, or ever again. We might not get a second chance.

Bumblebee, Centipede's wife, works especially hard to make the plants happy. She feels particularly bad about her husband's wrongful deed and forever goes from flower to flower uttering her appreciation to them. Her throat got so sore from singing to the flowers that all she can do now is buzz. And Potato Bug, Centipede's daughter, she mulches the dry leaves day and night to feed the plants and trees, which is why she is often tired and ornery.

And what of Centipede? Well, he's left on the ground singing to the golden poppy, who once was the young girl who made beautiful headdresses and is still his neighbor. He sings thus:

You cover the Mountain spring and summer

All admire your beauty

But none more than me.

Part 5

*A*fter Answer Woman finished telling the story about Centipede and his footrace, Question Woman became curious again, which, as you know by now, is her nature.

"Sister," Question Woman said, addressing her twin, "that is just a story. Are stories true?"

"Stories are true, my dear Sister—they are never *just* stories. They teach us what is most true about this wondrous Mountain. Stories, in fact, are how we can see what *is* true. They are like windows that we can look out of and see a part of the real world. And when you look out of one of these windows, that is, when you hear a story, you will find a true and everlasting lesson about that world—which of course is none other than the world of Sonoma Mountain, where you and I live. Oh, there are so many stories, so many true lessons."

"Like what?" asked Question Woman, who had already forgotten the story she had just heard about Centipede and his footrace.

"Stories teach us that we are all connected and equal on this Mountain—the humans, the plants and trees, birds, animals. The entire Mountain, everything you see, is really one ongoing story."

"What do you mean?" asked Question Woman.

"For example, if we only see a poppy as a flower, if we don't know its story, then we can't learn any lessons from it. If grass is just grass, or a rabbit just a rabbit, then what do we know? We know very little then...The big ongoing story is that each of us—the humans, the plants and trees, birds, animals—has a story to tell. For that reason we must respect all of life. When we forget this big ongoing story we get into trouble."

"Well then, Sister, what about rocks?" asked Question Woman. "Can they teach us stories too?"

"Oh my, yes," answered Answer Woman. "Rocks have spirits like anything else. They can teach us stories too. Listen to this one."

Lizard and Mockingbird Kidnap Rock's Daughters

*L*izard didn't always know about the weather, but he learned. Today, if you watch Lizard, you can know about the weather too. If it is going to be a very warm day, Lizard will be out just before sunrise. If the warm weather is going to change, if it is going to become cooler, Lizard will be looking west toward the ocean for the fog or rain clouds. Lizard has a song to help him know these things long before any others of us can know. But Lizard didn't always have this song. It belonged to Rock, a tall, handsome woman who lived at the village on Copeland Creek with her three bird daughters, Meadowlark, House Wren, and Finch.

Lizard lived there too. Lizard was an older man with graying hair and a pointed nose. He liked to eat mosquitoes and ticks. He used nets made of fern bracken to catch mosquitoes that hovered over the creek in summertime; and, to catch ticks in the fall after the first rains, he used a basket made of willow branches. One day he thought to himself, I am getting to be an old man. I am tired of having to set my nets about the creek every day during the summer for mosquitoes, and I am tired of walking about these hills with my willow basket every day after the first rains looking for ticks.

That was when he thought of Rock. She knew when it was going to be warm, which was when the mosquitoes would be above the creek water; and she knew when it was going to rain, which was when the ticks would crawl about in the hills. Oh, if only she would teach me her special weather song, thought Lizard, then I would not have to waste as much time and work as hard. If I knew when it was going to be warm, I would put up my fern bracken nets above the creek water only on those days. Likewise, if I knew in the late fall when it was going to rain, I would pack my willow basket into the hills only on those days.

Lizard went to the large house at the edge of the village where Rock lived with her three bird daughters. She invited him in and asked him to sit at her table. Being a gracious and generous woman, she offered him a cup of fine nettle tea. "This tea will make your eyes bright and your hair shiny," she told him. But when Lizard asked her for her special weather song, she bowed her head and didn't say a word.

As it turned out, Rock's three bird daughters were sitting in a corner preparing seed for a pinole. When they looked to the table and found their mother with her head bowed, they repeated, one after the other, "Lizard, our mother cannot give away her special weather song. She is forbidden to give up that special song. It is hers and hers only. Please do not ask again, for you know it is not in our gracious and generous mother's nature to refuse people." Three times he heard the message from Rock's daughters.

"All right then, I understand," Lizard said and left without taking any of the fine nettle tea Rock had so generously prepared for him.

He tried to think of another way to make his work easier but came up with nothing. All the while he became more and more frustrated thinking how much easier his work would be if only he had Rock's special weather song.

One day Lizard came upon Mockingbird gathering seeds on a hillside. Mockingbird was the stepdaughter of Coyote. She was known to be a bit of a schemer, like her stepfather, but she was nonetheless a very good worker. She was particularly good at gathering seeds.

"Mockingbird, I am in a predicament," said Lizard. "I am wondering if you could help me with something."

"What is the problem?" asked Mockingbird.

"You see I am getting to be an old man. It is harder for me to put up nets over the creek water for mosquitoes every day in the summer, and, after the first rains, it is harder for me to go about these hills every day with my heavy willow basket looking for ticks. If you will help me to get Rock's special weather song, I won't have to work every day. I will even be able to get more mosquitoes and ticks because if I know when it is going to be warm and when it is going to be cold I can put up more nets and pack an extra basket. And I can share some of my good catch with you—I know you like to eat bugs too."

"So what is your plan?" asked Mockingbird.

"There's really not much to it," answered Lizard. "If you will just tell Rock's three bird daughters that you know where there is an abundance of good seeds for pinole and then take them out of the village for a day, then I can ask Rock for that special weather song, which, being gracious and generous, she will give as long as her three protective daughters are not around to interfere."

"What happens when those three bird daughters find out that I am lying?" asked Mockingbird.

"Just tell them that you are lost. Go far on the other side of the Mountain."

Mockingbird thought of those fat mosquitoes and plump ticks and said, "Yes."

So early the next morning Mockingbird coaxed into the hills Rock's three bird daughters, Meadowlark, House Wren, and Finch. But before long, Rock's daughters became suspicious. After all, it was well known that Mockingbird, the stepdaughter of Coyote, was a trickster.

"Something is wrong here," said Meadowlark.

"Yes," responded House Wren, "Mockingbird said she was taking us to the far side of the Mountain, but why are we going the long way around instead of directly over the top?"

Finch agreed and said, "It is as if Mockingbird wants to keep us away from our home."

Mockingbird was walking quite a ways ahead of the three sisters and could not hear what they were saying. But when she saw the three sisters hesitate and then stop, she called out to them. "Come along. A huge patch of seed is just up ahead here." But what was up ahead was a deep crack in the earth, and when the three sisters approached the deep crack, Mockingbird pushed them inside and sealed the top with a big rock.

Meanwhile, Lizard went to Rock's house and asked again for her special weather song. Again, Rock, gracious and generous, gave him a cup of fine nettle tea that would make his eyes bright and his hair shiny. But once more Lizard did not drink the tea. He kept asking for Rock's special weather song, and each time Rock bowed her head and said nothing.

Because it was not in her nature to refuse people's wishes, Rock became more and more upset. She knew that she was forbidden to give away her special song, but she could no longer refuse Lizard. At last, she ran out of the house and tore out of the village to escape Lizard. He kept after her, all the while pleading with her to give him her song. Then on the west side of the Mountain, just below Round Oak Road, he got in front of her and stopped her in her tracks.

"Now give me your special weather song," he commanded.

When she looked up at him there was a beautiful light around her face, and she was smiling just as when she met him at her front door and offered him nettle tea. Her words floated forth soft as dandelion cotton.

"I will give you my song, but first I must tell you exactly what it does so that you will be able to know the weather before anyone else. When you sing the song, you will feel your ears open up. Your ears will not become bigger, only more sensitive. If it is going to be warm, you will feel heat in your ears. If it is going to be foggy or rainy, you will feel the cold. You only need to sing the song once, for then your ears will be fixed special forever." And then she began to sing thus:

It's not what I can see

That's not what I know

Coming to me

Coming to me on invisible wings

Lizard immediately began to sing this song. He felt a slight pop in his ears, like when he climbed to the top of the Mountain, and he knew then that his ears had been fixed. But when he looked back at Rock, he was alarmed to find that she had become stiff and hard. Already dried moss and lichen covered her. She would not move. Lizard commanded her to follow him back to the village. "You who do not refuse people, come with me," he said to her, but still she did not move. At last, Lizard went back to the village alone.

By this time it was approaching nightfall. Rock's three daughters had figured out what had happened. They knew that they had been kidnapped so Lizard could get their mother's special weather song. In that hole below the big rock they cried for their mother. Even though they were sad and crying, Mockingbird thought that they sounded beautiful. When Mockingbird pushed the big rock aside, the three bird sisters climbed out of the hole and raced back to the village. Alas, their mother was nowhere to be found, and again they cried and cried. They sat at the table where they used to sit with their mother and wept awfully, unable to console one another.

Passing the house on her way back into the village, Mockingbird heard them. Again, she thought they sounded beautiful, that they had lovely voices, and Mockingbird, who had no beautiful songs, and not a particularly good voice, saw an opportunity. She knocked on the door and then made the three sisters an offer. "You sound sad now, but you have beautiful voices, and I know you know many beautiful happy songs. If you teach me those happy songs and teach me to sing them beautifully, I will find your mother for you."

"No, we don't trust you," answered Meadowlark. "First you must tell us what happened to our mother. Where did Lizard take her?"

Both of Meadowlark's sisters, House Wren and Finch, agreed with her. "Show us where our mother is first," they told Mockingbird.

"Well, I guess you will never see your mother again," said Mockingbird as she started away from the three sisters. "Good-bye then, you poor motherless girls."

"Wait!" cried Meadowlark. "I will teach you my song and, if you sing just like I teach you, it will sound beautiful."

House Wren and Finch were perplexed. They couldn't believe their smart older sister would actually trust Mockingbird, the stepdaughter of Coyote. But when they heard her singing her song, teaching Mockingbird to sing the song completely off-key, they understood how truly smart their older sister was. They followed in the same manner, teaching Mockingbird to sing their songs completely off-key.

Mockingbird did not know the difference. She thought to

herself, Now I can sing beautifully. Then she found Lizard, and Lizard told her to bring Rock's three bird daughters to him and together they could all go to where he left Rock. "Something quite strange has happened," Lizard told Mockingbird before she left to fetch the three bird sisters.

So all of them went to the west side of the Mountain where Lizard left Rock. Even before they reached Rock, her three daughters could hear her singing thus:

My daughters

My daughters

My daughters

I am your mother

I am your mother

I am your mother

Meadowlark and House Wren and Finch saw how their mother had become stiff and hard and how she was covered with dry moss and lichen. Then suddenly where they had been standing there appeared three rocks, smaller but hard and lichen-covered just like the Rock mother.

"Oh, well, nothing we can do now," said Lizard. "At least Rock and her daughters are together again."

Then, at once, there was a beautiful chorus in the air. When Lizard and Mockingbird looked up, they saw the three bird sisters perched high on a pine branch.

"Yes, it is us, the three bird sisters," Meadowlark said.

House Wren said, "Lizard, you have taken our mother's heart and now she is still and cold. Her special weather song was her heart. You will know about the weather long before anyone else, but you will never again be able to leave our gracious and generous mother. At night, you will sleep under her. During the day, you will crawl about her, tickling her skin so she will once again laugh. Furthermore, since you didn't want what she had to offer, that good nettle tea to make your eyes bright and your hair shiny, you will have dull eyes and dry, hairless skin."

"Hey, I thought the three of you turned into rocks," Mockingbird shouted up to the three sisters.

Then Finch, the last of the three sisters, spoke. "Only our hearts have turned to stone. Our hearts will remain with our mother. As for you, Mockingbird, you will find that all you can do is imitate our beautiful songs, and thus you will sing like a fool all day and night for the rest of time."

Then Lizard went to Rock, and lo and behold, he found that Rock, gracious and generous, continued to protect him. Why? Because Lizard now had Rock's special weather song, which was her heart. As long as Rock's heart was close to her, she would act in the same gracious and generous manner she always had before. And Mockingbird found that her foolish singing kept Rock company through the night, reminding Rock of her daughters' great love for her. And, just at dawn when Mockingbird stops singing, the three bird daughters know it is time for them to wake and sing, and all the other birds gather around and join them.

Part 6

*T*he twin sisters, Question Woman and Answer Woman, kept talking. After Answer Woman told the story about Lizard and Mockingbird kidnapping Rock's three bird daughters, she was reminded of something else she needed to tell her sister about the stories and life on Sonoma Mountain.

"Remember when I said, 'If we only see a poppy as a flower, if we don't know its story, then we can't learn any lessons from it'?"

"I don't remember."

"Don't you remember I said, 'If grass is just grass, or a rabbit just a rabbit, then what do we know?' and I answered myself, 'We know very little then'?"

"Dear Sister, have you forgotten that I am Question Woman? Have you forgotten that I cannot remember a single story, which is why I must always ask you questions in order to hear the answers again?"

"Ah, yes, I guess I forgot," answered Answer Woman. "But in any event there is something else I must tell you about the animals and plants and their stories."

"And that is?" asked Question Woman.

"In addition to knowing each animal's story, we must see that in its story there will always be the stories of other animals too. In that way, we are reminded of how all of life on the

Mountain is connected, that in fact all of the stories together make up the one big ongoing story of the Mountain—the lesson we must never forget."

"I think I understand," said Question Woman, "at least for the moment."

"For example, in the story about Water Bug you can see other creatures' stories. Eagle is in Water Bug's story. Water Bug's story becomes part of her story too. Yes, even a creature seemingly as simple as Water Bug is connected to great creatures like Eagle and important to them."

"What is Water Bug's story?"

"It's the story of how Water Bug stole Water."

"Water is a creature too? A spirit like the others?"

"Oh, yes," answered Answer Woman. "Water is a most important spirit. Listen to the story."

Water Bug Walks Away with Copeland Creek

*T*his happened at the big village near the headwaters of Copeland Creek. Water Bug had lived there with his many grandchildren, years before his old wife had left him. He was a stout little old man with skinny short legs. Though he worked hard and helped his many grandchildren, he was often irritable, and people usually tried to avoid him. It wasn't just because he was old that he was irritable; he had been a rather unpleasant character all of his life. Some people said he went around mad because he was born short and had skinny legs. Other people said it was just his nature to be hotheaded. One morning, after he complained unmercifully about the pinole his old wife had served him for breakfast, she stood by the Creek and said aloud to the open sky, "How long do I have to put up with him?" And in that moment she rose into the sky and became an eagle, the greatest of soaring birds.

Many miracles happened there at the water's edge. Once a plain-looking lizard found himself with a blue tail there, and that is how Blue-Tailed Skink was born. And it was at the Creek's edge that Spider taught the people to weave beautiful baskets after a girl had gone to the Creek to fetch water for her sick grandmother. "I have no way to pack water back to my sick grandmother but with my cupped hands," the girl said. Spider stepped forth from the willows and said, "Don't cry, young girl. I will teach you to weave a basket so tight you will be able to pack water with it to your grandmother."

So the Creek was sacred to the villagers. Its water taught people many lessons about life, reminded people of many important stories, not least that every living creature needed water and thus was united by the Creek. Everyone needed water. Each morning people cleansed themselves in the Creek, starting the day with the water's blessings. They offered scraps of food to the water as well as songs and prayers in gratitude for the water's many gifts. They didn't want the beautiful flowing Creek to forget them.

One late fall day, before the rains, when the hills were very dry, Water Bug spied a woman bend down and drink from the Creek with her lips. It was Deer, and she was an attractive woman. Water Bug was resting under a good-sized bay laurel tree there. As he sat, he noticed that many people came and drank water, bending down and taking the water with their mouths. Of course this was not unusual, for he too often drank water from the Creek in this fashion. But he had never paid such close attention before; he had never sat so long watching others. He was amazed at how each person came and bent down and kissed the water. If only I could be Water, then everyone would kiss me, a crabby stout man with skinny legs, he thought. The idea was crazy and it made no sense—and Water Bug knew it. But when he saw Quail, the most beautiful woman of all, stoop and kiss the water, he lost his mind, for he could not stop thinking about her lovely soft lips on the water.

He stood up then and went to the Creek's edge and spoke thus: "Oh, I do not want to know all of your secrets, but only your song that enchants all to kiss you. I am an irritable old man with no wife, and I am short and stout with skinny legs. Certainly no one will kiss me without your song."

The Creek did not answer him.

Again he said, "Oh, I do not want to know all of your secrets, but only your song that enchants all to kiss you. I am an irritable old man with no wife, and I am short and stout with skinny legs. If I could just borrow your song for a while, I would be able to get someone to kiss me."

Still the Creek did not answer him.

"All right, have it your way, you old thing with moss on your edges," Water Bug said with utmost bitterness.

He walked off, but, as you might imagine, he was not satisfied. He kept thinking about Quail's lips, and he was determined to get the Creek's song. "I know what I'll do," he said to himself. "I'll kidnap the Creek and force him to give me his song. I'll hide him in a secret cave and starve him until he gives me his song."

Which is just what Water Bug did, but not until he had made careful plans. He had to make sure that no one saw him kidnap the Creek and that he had plenty of time to get to the far side of the Mountain with his prisoner. Since night was the best time to carry out this deed, Water Bug figured he would only have to worry about the folks who traveled about after dark, such as Raccoon, Bobcat, and Owl. An expert fire maker,

Water Bug called these night creatures together and offered to teach them how to make an enormous bonfire. Thus, while teaching these night fellows, Water Bug made an enormous bonfire around which they immediately began relaxing and telling one another stories.

Then Water Bug hurried off to the Creek. He built a dam and then pushed the dam closer and closer to the Creek's headwaters until he was able to fit all of the Creek's water in a carrying basket. Thus, with the water in his basket, he trudged to a secret cave on the far side of the Mountain.

"Now, will you give me your song that enchants all to kiss you?" he asked the water trapped in his basket.

Water said nothing.

"All right, have it your way," Water Bug said angrily. "No one will find you here and you will starve and die."

In the morning, the villages were alarmed to find that the Creek was gone. All that was left was a trail of sand and dry rocks.

"What has happened?" the villagers cried. "Have we offended our beloved Creek in some way?"

Days and nights went by and still the water did not return. The villagers stood on the dry sand and prayed. They offered good pinole and fine baskets and necklaces, and still there was no Water. "What are we going to do?" they wondered aloud. "We will die of thirst, each and every one of us, and the Mountain will turn to stone."

Meanwhile, Water Bug hiked to the secret cave each night

and asked Water for his song. Water, trapped inside Water Bug's basket, was growing smaller. Soon there would be nothing left of him. He would starve and die, just as Water Bug had said. He figured he had to give Water Bug his song, for if he did not, he would surely die, and then there would be no chance of him ever making it back to the village again.

"All right," he said at last, "I will teach you my song," and he sang thus:

Bending to me

You see your love

Bending to me

You see your wide open eyes

Everywhere I go

Everywhere I go

Like that

Like that

Hey-hey hey-hey

Then off went Water Bug with the song. However, nothing in the village changed. But then why would it? Water Bug had left Water trapped in that secret cave and forgot about him there. Soon it was winter and still there was no water in the Creek. It rained but the Creek remained a trail of sand and dry rocks, unable to collect the water that fell from the sky. The salmon hovered at the Creek's dry mouth near the Laguna de Santa Rosa, unable to make their way up the Creek to the village.

"I am starving," said Bear. "I have no salmon to eat."

"I am starving," said Blue Jay. "I have no nuts to eat. The acorn trees are drying up."

"I am starving," said Sparrow. "I have no seeds to eat. The grasses are all dried up."

"We are all starving," the villagers cried. "We are all starving, and we are dying of thirst."

They continued to pray and sing songs and make offerings to the Creek but to no avail. Each night Raccoon, Bobcat, and Owl made a big bonfire the way Water Bug had taught them, and everyone in the village gathered around the fire to discuss what they might do in order to bring Copeland Creek back. At one point, Raccoon remembered that the night before the Creek disappeared, Water Bug had offered to teach him and Bobcat and Owl how to build a huge bonfire.

"We have been tricked," Raccoon said.

"Yes," Bobcat said, "Water Bug kept us busy so that we would not see what he was doing."

"Certainly Water Bug walked away with Copeland Creek," Owl said.

Water Bug, sitting with the others by the fire, denied any wrongdoing. "Why would I want to kidnap the Creek?" he asked.

At that point, Quail stood up. "I'll tell you why you wanted to kidnap the Creek," she said. "So you could kiss me each morning, you terrible old man." Quail was furious, for each morning she had been enchanted by Water Bug.

Now Water Bug knew his secret was out. "All right," he said, "I will bring Water back to the Creek." When Water Bug got to the secret cave he looked inside the basket and found that there was only a single drop of water left. Hurrying with the basket, he ran to the creek. But, alas, when he emptied the single drop of water into the dry creek bed, nothing happened. The single drop of water rested in the tiny crevice of a rock.

"The Creek is so offended it won't flow," cried Quail.

But it was Eagle, Water Bug's former wife, who swooped down and said, "Remember, each spirit on this earth has a special song that gives it life and power. I bet that miserable old man Water Bug, my stout, skinny-legged ex-husband, has Creek's song."

"I do not have Creek's song," Water Bug said.

But Eagle would not believe him. She clutched him in her sharp talons and lifted him straight into the sky, so high that Water Bug not only saw his village far below but also the great length of Copeland Creek where the trees and grasses had turned yellow and brown and where villagers up and down the dry creek bed were starving and dying of thirst.

"Spit out the song," demanded Eagle. "Spit it out!"

Water Bug still denied he had water's song. He was still thinking of Quail's lips touching his.

"I have no patience with you," Eagle said, at which point she let go of Water Bug with one of her talons, causing him to gasp, expelling Water's song, which fell to earth as a single drop of water. That drop of water fell into the tiny crevice where Water Bug had left Water after he had dropped him out of the basket. That way, the two drops of water, one being Water and the other being Water's song, began to grow, and Copeland Creek flowed once more.

Meanwhile, Water Bug was still dangling from a single talon. Before Eagle was all the way back to earth, Water Bug fell, causing both of his skinny legs to bend so that his feet were pointing backwards.

The people of the village took no pity on him. Coyote, the chief, came forward, saying, "I think the proper punishment for Water Bug would be to feed him to the hungry salmon making their way back to our village right now."

And it was then that the Creek spoke to Coyote and all the people of the village.

"No, if you do that, if you kill Water Bug, you will forget what happened here. Better to forgive him and give him a job cleaning the water and guarding the Creek on late fall days when the water is low and someone might attempt to steal it away."

The people of the village agreed and thanked the Creek for the good advice. Water Bug went to the water then, and that is why in late summer and early fall you find him keeping watch over the Creek, gliding over the water's smooth surface, gliding backwards because his feet are still pointing in the opposite direction.

Part 7

One day Question Woman looked around and saw that the leaves were changing their colors. She was sitting on that fence along Gravity Hill with her twin sister, Answer Woman. From where they were seated they could see much of Sonoma Mountain, and all the way to the ocean. Nearby, the leaves on the oak trees were curling and turning brown. A clump of poison ivy had turned bright red. The grass on the hills was dry.

"Summer will be over soon," Question Woman said to her sister. "I hadn't noticed until now how the leaves are turning colors."

"Ah, dear Sister, you mentioned yesterday that the leaves are changing colors and soon autumn will be upon us. You forgot already that you told me. But then you do forget things. Don't feel bad. If you did not forget things, you would not be here to ask questions; and without your questions there would be no stories for me to share with you and everyone else. After all, I can only remember the stories when you need answers to your questions."

The sisters looked west and saw the sun had moved south, another sign of the season's change.

"It's a good thing we can see these signs," said Question Woman. "How else would we know when to start storing food for winter?"

"Oh, but there is another sign," answered Answer Woman. "It is a sign that you can hear."

"And what sign is that?" asked Question Woman.

"The sound of crickets at night. Just before the first signs of autumn that you can see—the changing colors, the dry hills, the weakening summer light—you will hear the crickets start singing at the bottom of the Mountain. They will start singing under the bridge that crosses Copeland Creek. Then, day after day, night after night, they will begin their march up this glorious Mountain. You will hear them first by the water, then partway up the Mountain, until weeks later they reach the top and all of the Mountain is alive at night with their song."

"I will have to listen tonight to see how far up the Mountain they have come," said Question Woman. "That is, if I don't forget by then."

"Oh, you will remember. You will hear them singing and remember. That's their gift—to let people know that autumn will soon be here. Even a blind person will know. When the crickets have reached the top of the Mountain, we must get out our storage baskets and start filling them with nuts and dried berries for the winter months."

"How do the crickets know when to start singing?"

"Well, it is all actually a gift from Rattlesnake."

"Sister, what do you mean?"

"Well, listen to the story and I'll tell you."

Rattlesnake Wins Hummingbird's Heart

*B*obcat had a beautiful daughter. She was Hummingbird. She was beautiful to look at, but what was most attractive about her was her heart. She was particularly kind to old people, often cooking good meals for them and carrying messages to their relatives in distant villages. It was said that Hummingbird was so beautiful that at times you could see a picture of a red heart on her chest, just below her throat.

"She will make the best wife," said Fox, a young suitor. "I will make her mine."

"Oh, she is the finest maiden in the village," said Skunk, another suitor. "Surely she will be my wife one day."

"Both of you are just dreaming," said Raccoon. "I have seen Hummingbird and indeed she will be my wife one day very soon."

Then Mountain Lion stepped forward, laughing. "Wait until she sees me. I am bigger and stronger than any of you and certainly I am the man Hummingbird will want to marry."

Each of the young suitors offered Bobcat great gifts in order that he might grant to one of them his beloved daughter's hand. Fox offered a cache of acorns. Skunk offered a basket of fresh blackberries, and Raccoon offered a flicker feather headdress. Then Mountain Lion came along and placed a bow and several arrows on Bobcat's porch.

"Hah!" Mountain Lion said. "What man would not want this bow and these fine arrows with obsidian points sharp enough to skin a wild plum."

Bobcat looked at the many gifts on his front porch. He felt like a wealthy man and enjoyed the display of goods. Unfortunately, his daughter was not taken with any of the four suitors, nor with any of their gifts to her father. The custom required that a maiden's father must return the gift of any suitor if the maiden did not marry him.

"I will not be able to have any of these gifts if you don't choose one of these suitors to marry," Bobcat lamented to his daughter.

The four suitors too were frustrated. They visited Bobcat's house each morning to see if he had taken one of the gifts. But not one of the gifts was taken inside. No suitor was selected.

"What is the matter with these young men?" Bobcat asked his daughter.

"Nothing," answered Hummingbird. "Nothing is wrong with any of them, but none of them appeals to me."

"Well then," said Bobcat, "I will call for a contest where each of them can demonstrate for you a special talent. Certainly one of these fine young men will appeal to you then."

Bobcat's idea was to have each of the young suitors perform a task with the gift that he had offered. That way his daughter would have to watch each of the young men perform and, thus watching, would fall in love with the most talented of them, the most suitable husband. Hummingbird agreed with this plan; in fact, she thought it was quite a good idea, but she asked that her father open the contest to all of the bachelors of the village. After all, there might be a fine young bachelor who had not yet made his talents known to Hummingbird.

Her father agreed, and the day of the contest arrived. All of the people from the village gathered in the wide meadow just below the top of the Mountain. There sat Bobcat and his lovely daughter Hummingbird at the front of the large crowd. Coyote, the chief of the village, and his wife Frog Woman were there too.

"Let the contest begin," exclaimed Coyote.

All of the contestants were hidden behind a thick stand of bay laurel trees. No one could see who was there, yet Bobcat and Hummingbird were certain that each of the four suitors was waiting.

The first suitor to come out from behind the trees was Fox. He carried his burden basket, which was filled with his cache of acorns. He emptied his acorns on the ground before Bobcat and Hummingbird, then tore off to the nearby oak trees and returned with another full basket, which he again emptied at the feet of Bobcat and Hummingbird. Over and over he returned with a full basket of acorns until there was a mound of acorns as wide as a house and twice as tall as a man.

"Beat that," he said to Skunk, who came forward next.

Skunk emptied his basket of blackberries. Then he hurried to a clump of blackberry vines and in no time was back with another full basket of berries. Again and again, he returned with a full basket of blackberries, emptying each basket until his pile of blackberries was twice the size of Fox's mound of acorns. By this time, Bobcat and Hummingbird could hardly see past the huge mounds and tell which contestant would come out from behind the trees next.

"I am here," Raccoon said, standing alongside the mound of berries. "Never mind these things to eat," he said, looking into the eyes of Hummingbird and holding up his flicker feather headdress. "I will make you something beautiful to behold."

Raccoon left and when he returned he had in his hands a flicker feather headdress that trailed nearly the length of the entire meadow. He boasted killing ten thousand flickers. When he rolled up the headdress it was the size of Skunk's blackberry mound.

"Ah, that's nothing," Mountain Lion said, stepping forward and pushing Raccoon aside. "Let us not forget it is autumn. The oak trees are full of acorns. The vines are full of berries. Everywhere flickers are in the trees. With my special gift and my talent I can make a mound twice the size of these mounds any day of the year."

Mountain Lion took the bow and fine arrows with sharp obsidian points that he offered Bobcat for Hummingbird's hand and went off. When he returned he was carrying two slain deer, which he dropped on the ground. Off he went again and again, until there were deer piled in a mound the size of the three other mounds together.

"Now you will have enough jerky for the entire winter,"

Mountain Lion boasted.

Indeed the crowd was impressed. Bobcat looked at his daughter. Nuts, berries, the headdress, the piled deer—the mounds surrounded her and she could not see past them. She seemed overwhelmed and confused, though Bobcat was certain she would announce her decision shortly.

"Are there any other contestants?" Coyote hollered over the mounds.

Bobcat saw that the four contestants, each standing in front of his hill of goods, were chuckling to themselves. At last they began to laugh out loud, and Bobcat had no idea what was so funny. He looked to his daughter and found that her eyes were upon a small, lowly fellow who had made his way around the mound of acorns. This fellow was Rattlesnake and he walked right up to Bobcat.

"I would like to vie for your lovely daughter's hand," he said.

The spectators all broke out in laughter. No one but Hummingbird had seen him come from behind the mound of acorns. He had a pleasant enough face but he was rather short and plain in appearance.

"You have offered me no gift yet that might impress my daughter," Bobcat said, attempting to mind his manners in front of this seemingly unworthy candidate. "What can you offer and what can you do?"

Bobcat looked at the four giant mounds that grew up like hills before the crowd, then looked back at Rattlesnake.

"I can offer a song that will call the crickets to the top of the Mountain," answered Rattlesnake.

"And what good is such a song?" asked Bobcat.

"Blind people and old people who are too feeble to leave the village will know that autumn is soon upon us. When they hear the crickets singing atop the Mountain they will know to check their provisions. They will know to make sure the young people of the village are packing the storage baskets, and they can dream of the oaks' curling brown leaves and the bright red color of poison ivy."

"But what good does such a song have for me?" responded Bobcat. "I am neither blind nor old."

Rattlesnake had no answer for Bobcat. The crowd laughed loudly again. All the while Rattlesnake stood respectfully before the unimpressed father and his lovely daughter.

Finally, Coyote, the chief, spoke. "Fair enough, Rattlesnake, sing your song and let's see what happens."

"Well, sir," Rattlesnake said, turning to Coyote, "there is just one problem. I can sing the song; but because the crickets are now below the bridge at the bottom of the Mountain, it will take them at least two weeks to reach the village here. I must go off and lead them this way with the song. But I promise the crickets will return with me."

"But we cannot sit here for two weeks," complained Bobcat.

Rattlesnake turned then to Bobcat. "We could meet back here in two weeks, if you would honor me with the privilege of offering my song and proving my talent. In the meantime, feed the people with this food and share the marvelous head-dress."

Again, Coyote, the chief, spoke. "Fair enough, Rattlesnake, we will meet you back here in two weeks' time. Do you have any problem with that plan, Bobcat?"

Bobcat thought the plan was ridiculous. What did he want with a thousand crickets singing? But he did not want to disrespect the headman, Coyote. "Fine," he answered.

Rattlesnake bowed his head, preparing to take leave of the large audience, and then started down the Mountain.

That was when Hummingbird, who had not said a single word the entire day, finally spoke.

"Rattlesnake," she said, "if you would not mind, I would like to hear your song before you leave."

"Oh, Hummingbird, if it pleases you I will sing," Rattlesnake answered her, and thus he began to sing:

> *Your brothers and sisters*
>
> *The stars*
>
> *On the mountaintop are calling for you*
>
> *The stars*
>
> *Your aunts and uncles*
>
> *On the mountaintop are calling for you*

The stars

Your old mother and father are there

On the mountaintop calling for you

The stars

The lost people of your village

On the mountaintop are calling for you

Then the plain little man left and the people returned to the village.

It is said that even before Rattlesnake had begun to sing his song, people could see that a picture of a red heart had appeared on Hummingbird's chest, just below her throat. Bobcat must have seen that heart too. Why else would he have said to Hummingbird that night, "Daughter, you will never marry Rattlesnake. Poor fool, he lives in a cave and has nothing worthwhile to offer."

Hummingbird certainly felt otherwise, yet she knew not to disagree openly with her father. She knew he would never permit her to marry Rattlesnake. She knew that, even though her father had not said as much, all along he intended for her to marry Mountain Lion. He was impressed with Mountain Lion's gift of a bow and arrows with obsidian points sharp enough to skin a wild plum, and then with the pile of deer Mountain Lion had slain. Mountain Lion was indeed the biggest and the strongest of Hummingbird's suitors, and she was certain that her father would not let anything get in the way of her marrying him—even if he had to kill Rattlesnake, who clearly her heart was set on.

That night, while her father slept, Hummingbird stole away. She went down the Mountain to find the one who had won her heart. When her father woke the next morning, he knew what had happened and was outraged. He called together the four suitors—Fox, Skunk, Raccoon, and Mountain Lion—and told them that Hummingbird was below the bridge that crosses Copeland Creek at the bottom of the Mountain. "Go there and get her," he commanded. "Whichever one of you brings her back to the village will win her hand."

So the four suitors raced down the Mountain. But, alas, when they reached the bridge, they found that Hummingbird had turned into a bird so small that she was able to hide behind a single bay laurel leaf high up in the tree. In fact, they would never have found her if they hadn't heard her singing and looked up. She was singing thus:

> *Beloved*
>
> *Curled by the round rock*
>
> *Beloved*
>
> *Up and down this Mountain*
>
> *Until the end of time we go*

She stopped singing then and looked down at the four suitors.

"None of you shall marry me. Do not hurt Rattlesnake. If he is harmed, you will never see either of us again, and you will never be able to hear autumn approaching and know for certain when to start filling your storage baskets for winter. Rattlesnake was not thinking of me or my father; he was thinking of the old and the blind, my favorite people, and thus he has won my heart. Now go and tell my father what I have said. And do not waste the piles of food and the beautiful headdress. Fill your winter baskets, and each year pay attention to the singing crickets. You will know when autumn is upon you, and that I am following my husband calling the crickets to the mountaintop."

Mountain Lion was the most disappointed, for he had been certain that he would win Hummingbird's heart. But, like the others, he understood what Hummingbird said. Her father was none too happy either, but he too understood his daughter's message. Immediately, the villagers packed their winter storage baskets with the mounds of nuts, berries, and meat. With the enormous feather headdress they made blankets for the old people and the blind. And to this day Hummingbird follows Rattlesnake all about. You can see the picture of a red heart below her throat. And sometimes you can see her soar down close to him as if to whisper in his ear her song:

Beloved

Curled by the round rock

Beloved

Up and down this Mountain

Until the end of time we go.

Part 8

*O*ne day when the sun was particularly bright and warm upon the Mountain, a beautiful red dragonfly glided in the air above the twin sisters, Question Woman and Answer Woman. The twin sisters were sitting in their usual spot atop the wooden fence on Gravity Hill. They had a view of the Mountain and the valley and all the way to the ocean. Soon another dragonfly appeared, and it was blue. Then, before long, several dragonflies were there, dancing in the air, dragonflies of every color: orange, yellow, green, silver and gold, even pink. Some of the dragonflies were striped; some were small and short, others large and long.

"Oh my goodness," commented Question Woman. "They are so beautiful. Why so many different colors?"

"Even you who forgets everything should remember the answer to that question," said Answer Woman. "It is because of our grandfather, of course. Coyote is the one who created this world, this Mountain. He is the headman, the leader of the big village near the headwaters of Copeland Creek."

"If he is so important, there must be many stories about him. Why haven't you told me stories about him yet?"

"Because you haven't asked," replied Answer Woman.

"Oh, yes, and you can't remember a story unless I ask."

"Yes, that's right."

"Well, it never ceases to amaze me how beautiful our world on this Mountain is. Our grandfather Coyote must be a pretty smart man to have created such a wondrous place for us to live."

"He is a smart man," said Answer Woman. "But he had to learn many things, like everyone else. The things you see can tell the story of something he learned. Thus, he created a world that we can always learn from even as we behold its beauty."

"What do you mean?" asked Question Woman.

"Take these beautiful dragonflies, for instance. Their beauty, their many colors, tell a story about Coyote."

"What is the story?" asked Question Woman.

"I'm thinking of the story now," Answer Woman answered.

Coyote Creates a Costume Fit for a Chief

Coyote was the headman of the big village near the headwaters of Copeland Creek. That was where the people lived in that ancient time when all of the animals and plants on Sonoma Mountain were still people. Coyote lived in a house near the center of the village with his wife Frog Woman. Each morning Coyote walked through the village checking that all of his villagers had made it safely through the night. He checked to see if anyone was sick. He asked the old people if they would have enough to eat for the day. If they needed something to eat, he asked the young women about the village to prepare a full basket of acorn mush, and he asked the young men to bring boiled fish and tender meat that the old people could chew easily. Frog Woman, Coyote's wife, was a Dreamer. Her dreams told her when and where the villagers needed to hunt and gather food. If in her dreams Frog Woman saw salmon running in the creek, she knew it was time for people to prepare their nets. If she saw ripe brown acorns in the oak trees, she knew it was time for people to take up their burden baskets. Each morning, if Frog Woman had revealed a dream to Coyote, he had to instruct the villagers accordingly, telling them to take out their nets or baskets or whatever it was they needed for the task at hand.

On and on it went like that, day after day. One morning,

Coyote wondered if the people even noticed him any longer. He wondered if they appreciated him. That particular morning all of the villagers had survived the night safely and no one needed any food. As Coyote walked through the village, he saw that people were going about their business. Women were trimming sedge roots for basket making; men, seated in a circle, discussed where on the Mountain to set their snares for rabbits. Old men and women tended the children, telling stories and teaching important lessons. They don't want anything and therefore they don't notice me, Coyote thought to himself. They don't know—or even care!—that I am their chief passing by. He went to look for his wife Frog Woman. When he found her alongside the creek leeching acorn meal, he was alarmed to find that she didn't look up from her work either.

Then he went to see his nephew Chicken Hawk. Coyote and Chicken Hawk talked often and about many things. Though Chicken Hawk was younger than Coyote, Chicken Hawk was quite smart and Coyote sought his advice on many matters. Chicken Hawk, who had been preparing a bone whistle, saw his uncle coming.

"Uncle, why the sad look on your face this glorious morning?" asked Chicken Hawk.

Coyote told his nephew his thoughts. "The villagers don't appreciate me. I walk about, and unless they need something from me, they don't even look up to say hello."

"Ah, but I cannot believe that the villagers don't appreciate you," said Chicken Hawk. He then held up the bone whistle in his hand. "Look, Uncle," he said, "is this whistle not for the dance to honor you this evening? Didn't Frog Woman tell you just yesterday that it was time for your honoring dance, that we had only two days to get ready, me to prepare this bone whistle and Cricket to ready his voice? And you—you must sing the Chief's Song, which I must accompany with my whistle and Cricket with his voice."

"Oh, we have that dance every year," lamented Coyote. "It is no longer any more meaningful to the people than I am."

"You mustn't say that, Uncle," advised Chicken Hawk. "It isn't good to talk that way."

"I didn't come to you for a lecture," said Coyote. "In fact, I came to you to ask a favor."

"Well, what do you need?" asked Chicken Hawk.

"You have excellent eyes and you soar above the Mountain knowing the location of many secret things. I need to know where the Sun keeps his paints, all those colors that are iridescent, and I need to find a coat, the front of which is the blue of the midday sky, and I want a rattle that calls the attention of anyone passing by, and, finally, I want a hat that everyone will take notice of, the most distinct hat in the land."

"Uncle, you wish to create a costume fit for a chief," Chicken Hawk said.

"Yes," answered Coyote. "How did you know?"

Chicken Hawk did not like this idea of his uncle's at all. But before Chicken Hawk could speak what was on his mind, Coyote commanded, "Off with you, Nephew. Bring me the secret things that I want." Given Coyote was his elder and headman, Chicken Hawk left to do what he was asked.

First, Chicken Hawk went to the Sun and spoke thus: "Mighty Old Father, I have been sent by my uncle, the headman of our village, to take the paints you hold so dear. Flying over this Mountain, I know where you keep those beautiful colors—in a crevice just below the highest ridge—but I would never think of taking them without asking you first."

"You are a good and decent fellow," spoke the Sun. "Coyote is fortunate to have a nephew such as you. You may have my iridescent colors, but please leave enough of each color so that I can still paint the sky each morning. Oh, and one more thing: When you take the colors, please sing the first verse of your uncle's song, the Chief's Song, so that the song will accompany the paints back to your village."

Chicken Hawk obliged the Sun and thanked him for his generosity. Then he went and gathered a handful of each iridescent color from the secret crevice below the highest ridge. On the way back to his village, with the paints tucked under his arm, Chicken Hawk sang the first verse of his uncle's song:

Soundless like the wind

I pass by you

Lifting, lifting

I'm here

Dancing for you

Next Chicken Hawk went to a grove of bay laurels where a coat the front of which was the blue of the midday sky was hanging between two large branches of an old tree. The front of this coat was so blue that if you were to pass by you might not notice it but think instead that you were merely seeing between the two large branches to the sky. But Chicken Hawk knew the coat was there and to the old tree he spoke thus: "Honorable Mother, I have been sent by my uncle, the headman of our village, to take the coat you hold so dear. Flying over this Mountain, I have seen where you keep this coat, the front of which is the color of the midday sky—hanging between your two large branches—but I would never think of taking it without asking you first."

"You are a good and decent fellow," spoke the old Bay Laurel tree. "Coyote is fortunate to have a nephew such as you. You may have my coat hanging between my two large branches, but beware: The seams on each side are stained from having rubbed against the branches for so long, through many wet winters. Do not try to remove the stains. Oh, and one more thing: When you take the coat, please sing the second verse of your uncle's song, the Chief's Song, so that the song will accompany the coat back to your village."

Chicken Hawk obliged the old Bay Laurel tree and thanked her for her generosity. Then he plucked the coat from between the tree's two large branches, noticing that indeed the two seams were stained. The coat was very heavy and Chicken Hawk had to carry it over his shoulder. On the way back to his village, packing the coat thus, he sang the second verse of his uncle's song:

Strong like the wind

I pass by you

Rain and hail at my back

I'm here

Covering you

Then Chicken Hawk went to a large cave on the east side of the Mountain where a rattle that called attention to anyone passing by was hidden. Stairs made of rocks led to the Cave's opening. Chicken Hawk climbed and climbed. At the top of the stairs he spoke to the Cave thus: "Oh, wise Brother, I have been sent by my uncle, the headman of our village, to take the rattle you hold so dear. Flying over this Mountain, I know where you keep that rattle—on the floor inside your rock walls—but I would never think of taking it without asking you first."

"You are a good and decent fellow," spoke the Cave. "Coyote is fortunate to have a nephew such as you. You may have my rattle that can call attention to anyone passing by, but please carry it carefully. Don't drop it. Oh, and one more thing: When you take the rattle, please sing the third verse of your uncle's song, the Chief's Song, so that the song will accompany the rattle back to your village."

Chicken Hawk obliged the Cave and thanked him for his generosity. Then he went into the Cave and found the rattle. On his way back to the village, with the rattle held firmly in his hand, he sang the third verse of his uncle's song:

Like the wind, nothing much for the eye to see

I pass by you

Rattling, rattling

I'm here

Warning enemies for you

Finally, Chicken Hawk went to a small spring where the most distinct hat in the land was hidden. This amazing hat was shaped like a feather. To the Spring he spoke thus: "Kind and beautiful Sister, I have been sent by my uncle, the headman of our village, to take the hat you hold so dear. Flying over this Mountain, I know where you keep the hat that everyone would take notice of—amidst the ferns where your water bubbles from the earth—but I would never think of taking it without asking you first."

"You are a good and decent fellow," spoke the Spring. "Coyote is fortunate to have a nephew such as you. You may have my hat, but please handle it with great care. Oh, and one more thing: When you take the hat, please sing the fourth verse of your uncle's song, the Chief's Song, so that the song will accompany the hat back to your village."

Chicken Hawk obliged the Spring and thanked her for her generosity. The hat was lovely to behold. Holding it carefully with both hands, Chicken Hawk headed back to the village. All along the way he sang the fourth verse of his uncle's song:

A gentle wind

I pass you by

Touching the huts' walls

I'm here

Even as you sleep

Coyote was pleased. On his table sat all of the things he had asked Chicken Hawk to find: colors that are iridescent, a coat the front of which is the blue of the midday sky, a rattle that calls the attention of anyone passing by, and a hat that everyone would take notice of.

"Chicken Hawk, you have done well," Coyote told his nephew.

"Yes, it is my duty to honor you, Uncle. But there has been something on my mind ever since you asked me to find you these secret things. If you would permit me, I would like to tell you what I think about your creating a costume fit for a chief."

Coyote, already dazzled by his new possessions, said, "There isn't anything for you to tell me. I know already about the costume I shall create. I see it clearly in my mind."

"Well then, Uncle, please allow me to tell you the rules for each of the things you will use to make the costume."

"You may tell me, but be quick for I am anxious to get started," said Coyote.

"You must use only the paint you have, no more. Do not attempt to remove the stains from the coat. Never drop the rattle. Make sure to handle the hat with great care."

"Is that it?"

"Yes, Uncle."

"Well, I have one more thing to ask you. You mustn't tell anyone about this costume I am going to create. Just go with the others to my honoring dance tomorrow night and wait for me there."

Chicken Hawk obliged his uncle then left. Coyote went to work on his costume straight away; he wanted to be finished and out of the house before Frog Woman returned, for he wanted to surprise her too.

He put on the coat and affixed the rattle to its collar. Next he painted his face with the iridescent colors and then plopped the hat on his head. But he was greatly dissatisfied. "Look," he said to himself, "this coat is stained along its seams, the rattle is so small no one will see it let alone hear it, the paint hardly reaches to my chin, and the hat, rather than being square, curves to the side. Instead of distinguishing myself so people will notice me as their chief, I will only be laughed at."

He thought of summoning Chicken Hawk to find him some different things for his costume. But there was not enough time. Coyote grew more and more frustrated, and he knew that Frog Woman might come through the door at any minute and find him in that silly costume. He had to think fast. He took off the coat and rattle and he stripped the paint from his face and pulled off the hat. He found a brush and scrubbed at the stains on the coat. He tossed the rattle to the floor and rolled it under his foot to make it longer. He added water to the paint so that when he painted his face again the iridescent colors covered his chin and reached to his neck. He tugged and pulled on the hat, attempting to make it square. Then, just before Frog Woman reached the house with her leeched acorn meal for supper, Coyote stole away. He hid in a thicket of willows and waited for night to come. Some stains remained on the coat, the rattle wasn't much larger, the paint was somewhat fainter in color, and the hat still curved to the side, but Coyote was satisfied.

"Where is my husband?" asked Frog Woman when she found only his empty seat at the dinner table.

"Where is Coyote?" asked Cricket. "Coyote is supposed to lead us into the ceremonial brush house for his honoring dance, and I am supposed to sing and Chicken Hawk is supposed to play his bone whistle."

Chicken Hawk was standing there with all of the people waiting outside the ceremonial brush house for Coyote. But, keeping his promise to Coyote, he said nothing of his uncle's whereabouts or what he was up to.

At long last, everyone went into the brush house. They figured Coyote would find them. Coyote never showed up. The people became worried and then frightened.

"I fear that whatever has happened to my husband isn't good," said Frog Woman.

"We no longer have a chie!" exclaimed Cricket. "What are we to do?"

And just then, as Cricket finished speaking, there appeared in the doorway a most monstrous figure. The people gasped and pushed back from the center of the room. Then slowly the horrible-looking creature made its way toward the fire.

"We are cursed by a demon!" Cricket shouted.

Shadows from the fire danced across the blue-fronted coat. People could see the rattle hanging from the coat's collar. The glistening paint covered the eyes and sealed the lips. The top of the hat seemed wilted, curving to the side.

Coyote made it only halfway to the fire in the center of the room, and then he collapsed. The coat had grown heavy, squeezing him, slowly but surely taking the last breath out of him. The rattle had seized his heart. The iridescent paints had glued his eyes and lips shut, and the hat was twisting his neck to its breaking point.

People screamed, pushed closer to the walls. Then, just before Coyote was to take his last breath, his body spasmed, heaving so violently that his costume flew into the air.

"It's Coyote!" people exclaimed.

"My husband!" Frog Woman cried.

Coyote rose to his feet and looked around. He saw the people gathered for his honoring ceremony. He was shocked and ashamed. "I must sing my Chief's Song," Coyote said to himself. But when he opened his mouth to sing there came from his throat only a long and sad howl.

"Uncle, maybe now you will listen to me," Chicken Hawk said, stepping forward. "You have broken the rules of the secret objects you wanted for your costume."

"But what of my Chief's Song?" asked Coyote.

Chicken Hawk turned to look at the crowd and Coyote did the same. The coat had landed on an old man, Lizard, and its front the blue of the midday sky looked brilliant below Lizard's wrinkles and gray hair. The rattle landed at the feet of a hardworking but rather ordinary-looking young man, Rattlesnake, and the rattle distinguished him from all of the other young men in the brush house. The hat fell atop the head of the kind young maiden Quail, and the hat, curving to the side, accented her beauty. And the paint splattered on a poor widow and her several children. That was Dragonfly, and it was the beautiful red paint that colored her, and the other iridescent paints colored each of her children, one by one.

"But where is my song?" Coyote asked again. "How can I be the chief without that song?"

"That's what I tried to tell you," Chicken Hawk said. "All that you ever needed to be chief was your Chief's Song. You did not need a fancy costume to show off. You were doing just fine. Everyone appreciated you. Your song was enough to remind them of your good actions and leadership should they ever forget."

"Oh, I have been a fool," lamented Coyote, ashamed and embarrassed. "I suppose I am not your chief anymore for I have lost my song."

Frog Woman stepped forward then. "Dear Husband, have you forgotten I dreamed two nights ago of this honoring ceremony for you? How could I have had that dream if you are not to continue as our chief?"

"Uncle," Chicken Hawk addressed Coyote, "the song is attached to the secret objects you requested. The song will remain with us that way as a reminder of your good deeds and the lesson that you have learned."

"Yes," said Frog Woman, "let the Chief's honoring ceremony begin!"

Cricket readied his voice to accompany the Chief's Song. Chicken Hawk picked up his bone whistle. Then the Widow Dragonfly and her several children of all sizes and shapes stepped forward and sang:

> *Soundless like the wind*
>
> *I pass by you*
>
> *Lifting, lifting*
>
> *I'm here*
>
> *Dancing for you*

Then it was Lizard's turn:

> *Strong like the wind*

I pass by you

Rain and hail at my back

I'm here

Covering you

Then Rattlesnake:

Like the wind, nothing much for the eye to see

I pass by you

Rattling, rattling

I'm here

Warning enemies for you

And, finally, Quail sang the fourth verse:

A gentle wind

I pass you by

Touching the huts' walls

I'm here

Even as you sleep

The ceremony turned out beautifully and the people felt safe and happy once again. Still, though, Coyote sometimes remembers his foolishness and late at night, when he thinks the rest of us are sleeping, he will howl in shame.

Part 9

*A*gain it was an autumn day and the twin sisters, Question Woman and Answer Woman, were perched atop the fence on Gravity Hill. They could see the hills that looked like steps to the top of the Mountain. Looking west, in the other direction, they could see the long stretch of valley below the Mountain, and further still the ocean where the Sun was low in the sky. Night was coming, and birds were flying across the golden light to their roosts. Long shadows spread over the land.

"This is a beautiful time of day," observed Question Woman. "I wish that the day would stay like this forever, bright and warm. But the sun is sinking lower and lower, and soon it will be night. And there are long shadows across the land and the leaves are changing colors, and soon it will be winter, and cold."

"Yes," said Answer Woman. "Nothing stays the same on this wondrous Mountain, not the time of day, not the seasons. Everything changes."

"Why?" asked Question Woman.

"Because without change we would forget that we are alive. Without feeling hot and cold, how would we know that we are feeling anything at all? If we couldn't hear the changes in people's voices, how would we know if they are happy or sad? If we couldn't see the grasses and trees and all of the other creatures on this Mountain changing, we might not notice them and then forget them. Then we would forget our place on this Mountain—we would forget who we are...And if there was not day or night, how would we know when to work and when to rest? We might work all the time or sleep all the time. Change lets us see and feel. And isn't it change that gets us to ask questions the way you just did?"

"Hey, Sister, aren't I the one who is supposed to ask the questions?"

"Ah, you just remembered who you are because there was a change. See what I mean?"

"Yes, I suppose. Well then, I have another question. How did night come about in the first place, and why do some creatures go about in the dark?"

"That's two questions, but I can give you the answer with one story. Listen."

Skunk Unleashes
the Night

*O*ne fall season there was a particularly good harvest of acorns. All of the different Oak trees were dropping an abundance of nuts. The people of the big village near the headwaters of Copeland Creek were working without stopping; in those days people did not stop working until a job was finished, for there was not yet Night and no set time to sleep. People finished a job, and only then did they sleep.

"We have been working for a thousand hours," said Moth.

"No," said Raccoon, "I think we have been working for two thousand hours."

"Two thousand hours, heck," said Owl. "It's been at least three thousand hours."

"Well, I think it's been four thousand hours," said Gray Fox, "and I'll tell you this: My muscles are so tired I could fall to the ground and sleep right now."

Coyote, who was chief, overheard these remarks. He commanded the people to keep working. "We must not waste this good harvest of acorns," he said. "There might come a time when we need every last one of these nuts to eat. Have you already forgotten that day some time ago when we nearly ran out of food? We must be prepared for such a time again and take advantage of what the oak trees are giving us."

Skunk was listening nearby. He was very tired also; his

back hurt from bending over the ground for so long. Then he got an idea and called out to Coyote. "Kind headman," he said, "you see that the Valley Oak gives the largest acorns. Why don't we just gather the acorns from the Valley Oaks and leave the acorns from the other trees? Kind headman, as you can see there are enough large acorns to feed the village for a long, long time."

"I think Skunk has the right idea," said Moth.

"I agree," said Raccoon.

"Me too," said Owl.

"And I think Skunk is right too," said Gray Fox. "Besides, we'll never be able to finish gathering the acorns from all of the trees."

Coyote considered what Skunk had proposed. Then, while Coyote was thinking about Skunk's idea, Squirrel came forth and said, "Though the acorns from the White Oaks are smaller, they make the sweetest mush."

And then Pileated Woodpecker chimed in. "And though the acorns from the Live Oaks are the smallest yet and difficult to husk, they make the best bread."

And Blue Jay stepped forward, saying, "And let us not forget that if we run out of acorns we will be forced to make mush and bread from buckeyes. If you think packing acorns is hard, try packing those big, hard buckeye balls. And buckeyes are not as good to eat..."

"And much harder to leach," said Frog Woman, Coyote's wife.

"Ah, my kind villagers," Skunk countered, "you can make the Valley Oak mush sweet by adding dried blackberries, and you can make good enough bread from the Valley Oaks' acorns by adding simply a drop of venison fat."

Coyote thought that Skunk offered a good argument, and he was about to agree with Skunk's idea of collecting only the large acorns from the Valley Oaks. But then Chicken Hawk, Coyote's nephew, came forward and said, "Ah, but Skunk, you are forgetting the sacred rule, which is that we must always take what the Oak trees offer no matter how tired we get or what ideas we think up on our own. Remember that if we don't appreciate the Oak trees they will forget us."

Chicken Hawk, though quite young, was wise, and Coyote knew to listen to his advice. "You are right," said Coyote. "The people must respect all of the Oak trees and keep working to gather the acorns they offer."

Skunk wasn't happy, but he didn't offer any further argument. He knew that Chicken Hawk was right. However, as time went on and he became more and more tired, he thought of something else. Only this time he did not share his idea with all of the villagers. He convened a secret meeting with his supporters, Moth, Raccoon, Owl, and Gray Fox. They gathered behind a large Bay Laurel tree low on the hill where the others couldn't see them. Skunk unveiled his idea there.

"Listen," he said. "We are working too hard and Coyote does not listen to us. He only listens to Chicken Hawk. We must follow my plan and only gather acorns from the Valley

Oaks, not the other Oak trees."

"But what about the sacred rule?" asked Moth.

"Oh, who cares about the sacred rule?" answered Skunk. "What difference does it make if the White Oaks and the Live Oaks forget us and no longer offer their acorns? We have plenty of nice big acorns from the Valley Oaks. We don't need the White Oaks and Live Oaks. Remember, if we want sweet acorn mush we can always add dried blackberries, and if we want to make bread from the Valley Oaks' acorns all we need to do is drop in a dollop of venison fat."

"Well," said Raccoon, "we cannot just stop working. The villagers will mock us and Coyote will punish us."

"Yes," said Gray Fox. "As tired as I am, I certainly don't want to be laughed at or called lazy."

"Ah, my friends," answered Skunk. "You haven't even listened to all of my plan. I have a great idea...Listen: We will disappear."

"What do you mean?" asked Moth.

"There is a secret cave near the bottom of the Mountain, not too far from the creek. We will go there and hide. Soon Coyote and the villagers will become exhausted and find that they cannot gather all of the acorns and they will have to compromise and gather only those from the Valley Oaks. Then everyone will see that what I said was right, and we won't have to work so long and hard."

"But there are only four of us," said Raccoon. "Five counting you, Skunk."

"We must share our plan with others who we think will agree with us," said Skunk.

They wondered if Skunk was right—that if they went and hid in a cave, Coyote would listen to them. They wondered too if others would follow them.

As it turned out, many people did follow them—in fact nearly half of the villagers—and thus they were greatly encouraged. "Skunk must be right," they said to themselves, stealing away down the Mountain. "Look how many of the villagers are following us."

Indeed, many people disappeared, leaving their burden baskets under the trees as if they were simply going to the creek for a drink of water, but then never coming back. Some people, like Deer and Mountain Lion, were undecided and only went halfway down the Mountain.

"Look here," said Skunk, rolling away a large white rock.

There for all to see was the secret entrance to the Cave.

"How in the world did you learn about this cave?" Gray Fox wondered aloud.

"One day as I was passing by here I heard voices. A woman was arguing with her daughter. Pressing my ear against this white rock, I knew that the woman and her daughter were inside a cave behind the rock."

Skunk led his followers inside the Cave. There was no woman there, but, alas, after Skunk and his friends had been there a few hours they discovered that the Cave was herself a woman, for they heard a lovely voice speak thus: "I will shelter you but only under one condition. You must never take my daughter outside, for if she is set loose in the world things will never be the same. She lives in a tiny leather satchel next to a small rock near the back of the Cave. She will tell you all kinds of things in order to persuade you to take her out of the Cave, but do not listen to her."

Skunk and his friends agreed. The Cave kept the people warm, and a lot of time passed.

"Coyote and his friends must be exhausted by now," said Moth. So much time has passed and they must see they can't gather the acorns from all of the Oak trees, but only from the Valley Oaks."

Skunk then called Owl, saying, "You are a good messenger and you have very good eyes. Go to Coyote and his loyal villagers and ask if they are ready to surrender. Keep your eyes open and report back to me everything that you see there."

Owl did what he was told. When he returned, he told Skunk what he had seen—a terrible sight indeed. Coyote and his loyal villagers were exhausted, completely worn out; some of them had collapsed onto the ground, unable to work any longer. Huge piles of acorns lay under the Oak trees—under the Valley Oaks as well as under the White Oaks and Live Oaks, for but a few people were still able to gather any acorns.

"Well then," said Skunk, "Coyote must be ready to surrender."

Owl looked down then, for he had to tell Skunk what he did not want to hear: "Coyote told me to tell you that he would never surrender."

"Oh, Coyote still listens to Chicken Hawk," Skunk said. "We will wait here longer, and then he will have to surrender. He and his friends will all collapse on the ground. If we must, we will take over the village then."

"Ah, but I must tell you something else," reported Owl. "You told me to keep my eyes open. After I left Coyote, I hid behind a pine tree and saw that some of Coyote's followers were preparing their bows and arrows for war."

"Oh, that's ridiculous," Skunk said. "Coyote and his friends are too tired to fight. Besides, how are they ever going to find us hidden in this cave?"

"What happens if they do find us?" Moth asked.

"I told you: They will be too tired and weak to fight," answered Skunk.

There was nothing to do in the Cave, so as Skunk and his friends waited they spent a lot of time sleeping. After all, the Cave was warm and dark, and the Cave never did speak again; they never again heard the lovely voice. So Skunk thought he was dreaming when he heard a woman singing thus:

Chicken Hawk, with the best eyes of all

Combs this Mountain

Chicken Hawk, with the best eyes of all

Walks down this Mountain

Chicken Hawk, with the best eyes of all

Approaches

Skunk woke with a startle. He had been sleeping near the back of the Cave, and when he looked about he found that he was next to a small rock. The tiny leather satchel was there.

"At last you have found me," the satchel spoke. "I can help you." The voice, the same that Skunk had heard singing, was soft and lovely, the voice of a fair young maiden.

"You are the Cave's daughter."

"Yes. But listen: Coyote has sent his nephew Chicken Hawk to find you. If you will but take me outside, I can fix things so that Chicken Hawk will be lost forever. Take me outside and unfasten the string that keeps the satchel tied. Once unleashed, I will cover the sky in darkness...I am Night."

"I've never heard of you," said Skunk.

"Of course not. My mother keeps me in this satchel, hidden away."

"But she said never to take you outside."

"She tells people all kinds of things. She even says that I stink. She is selfish. She doesn't want to live alone here. And me, I'll just end up a lonely old maid...Now listen: Take me out of here and we both win, I will find a husband and you will win your war with Coyote."

"But your mother said she wouldn't shelter us if we took you outside."

"Why would you need shelter if the sky is dark and no one

can find you? Honestly, Skunk, a leader needs to think clearly, and right now you are not thinking very clearly."

Skunk suddenly felt proud: He was a leader. "Okay," he said. "How do we get out of here?"

"My mother's eyes are near the entrance of the Cave. Put me under your tail and we'll go out that way. And make sure you barely open the rock door, lest you wake her."

So, with the tiny leather satchel tucked under his tail, Skunk left the Cave. Then, Skunk reached for the satchel and untied the string. All at once there was a loud explosion and a foul-smelling stench filled the air all around Skunk.

Moth, Raccoon, Owl, and Gray Fox pushed away the white rock in front of the Cave and came rushing out to see what had happened.

"Oh my goodness!" cried Moth. "Skunk has disobeyed the Cave and let loose her daughter!"

"The whole place stinks!" cried Raccoon, holding his nose.

"And look what happened to Skunk!" cried Owl.

They all looked and found Skunk, frustrated, struggling to detach the smelly satchel from under his tail. And that wasn't all. Down Skunk's back was a white line from where he had scratched himself while creeping past the barely-opened white rock door.

Behind them the Cave echoed, "I told you never to take my daughter outside. Now the world will never be the same."

"But where is your daughter?" asked a bewildered Gray Fox. "Where is Night?"

"Look up," answered the Cave. When everyone looked up, they found that the sky was dark, and not just the sky but everything around them, for Night had escaped and covered the entire Mountain in darkness.

Meanwhile Skunk kept trying to detach the satchel from under his tail, and he had discovered the white stripe down his back. "Look what has happened to me," cried Skunk.

But that was the least of his problems. Now the whole world was covered by Night. All of Skunk's followers came out of the Cave then and joined the four others gathered around Skunk. They pleaded with Night to return to the tiny satchel, but to no avail. She was free now and she ignored their pleas.

"What are we going to do?" said Moth. "Isn't there *anything* we can do to capture Night and put her back in the satchel?"

"Maybe if her mother calls her she will return," said Raccoon.

But even when the lonesome Cave begged her daughter to return, nothing happened. Night continued to cover the Mountain. Soon the trees all lost their leaves. The grasses stopped growing. Before long all of the villagers found them-selves wandering about in the darkness with nothing to eat. They became thin and pale without the sun, starving to death.

"You got us in trouble," Moth said to Skunk.

"Yeah, we should never have listened to you in the first place," said Raccoon.

"Now we are all going to die," said Owl.

"The world is going to end this way," said Gray Fox. "I want to go back to the village and see my relatives and friends there one last time."

"Yes," said Moth, "maybe Coyote can figure out how to get us out of this mess."

"We will have to tell Coyote we are sorry," said Raccoon.

"We'll have to plead forgiveness," said Owl.

"And tell Coyote that he was right and that Skunk was wrong," said Gray Fox.

And that was what happened. The weary congregation plodded back up the Mountain to the village. Shameful Skunk trailed behind. They found the village cold and the people there starving. Stacks of rotted and moldy acorns lay under the barren Oak trees. Nothing grew. No birds sang. The Mountain was dying.

"Look what has happened," Coyote said after both congregations had joined together in front of the empty ceremonial house. "I warned you. My nephew Chicken Hawk was right. Those of you who followed Skunk disobeyed the sacred rule, which is that we must always take what the Oak trees offer—all of the Oak trees. Then you went off. We even forgot one another then, for we found ourselves preparing for war, brother against brother, sister against sister. And that led to even more trouble, so that now Night is set loose and the Mountain is dying. We will die with the Mountain too."

"Oh," lamented Skunk, "I beg your forgiveness, Coyote. But isn't there anything you can do so that we don't all die?"

"We are punished. I don't know what we can do," answered Coyote.

Then Coyote's nephew Chicken Hawk came forward, and he had an idea. "Dear Uncle," he said, addressing Coyote, "perhaps you could go to the Sun and ask him how to use his iridescent colors to paint over Night and thus return light to the Mountain. Remember, Uncle, that the Sun is the oldest child of you and Frog Woman. If he will listen to anyone, Uncle, he will listen to you."

"But Chicken Hawk, where is the Sun? Where has he gone?"

"Well, I'm certain he is hiding now with his beautiful colors in that crevice just below the highest ridge of this Mountain. Go there and call him out."

Coyote left the village then and walked in the dark to the highest ridge of the Mountain. Standing over a small crevice there, he called to his eldest child, the Sun, and asked for help. "The Mountain is dying," Coyote said. "Night has covered everything. Can't you use your beautiful colors to paint the sky once again?"

"Dear Father Coyote," answered the Sun, "I could paint the sky, but not without the permission of all of the Oak trees. I must answer to them first because they were the first offended by the villagers. That is my rule."

"Well, would you please see what they have to say?" Coyote said. "Offer my apology on behalf of my villagers who broke the trees' sacred rule."

The Sun went off and convened a meeting with all of the Oak trees—the Live Oaks, the White Oaks, and the Valley Oaks. Then he returned to Coyote, who was sitting alone, waiting on the top of the Mountain.

"Dear Father," the Sun said, "the Oak trees are indeed greatly offended, and Skunk and his errant followers have brought a great catastrophe upon our beloved Mountain. The Mountain will never be the same. But the Oak trees have offered a compromise with special conditions. They will allow light to return only half of the time; Night will prevail the other half. And that is only if the Oak trees are cared for both while it is light and while it is dark, which means certain of the villagers will have to work from here on in the dark, while the rest continue to work in the light as before. That is what the Oak trees said, Father."

Coyote went back to his village then and relayed what the Oak trees had told the Sun. The villagers could do nothing but accept the Oak trees' offer; only that way would the Sun be able to use his brilliant colors and return light to the Mountain. And then, before the Sun painted the sky again, he painted Twilight, a handsome young man who would sing thus to the maiden Night again and again until the end of time:

Reaching for you

Touching you now

My hand in yours

We walk together until dawn

Night was content. Light returned. There was day. And

the Mountain returned to life. The trees grew leaves. Grasses grew and reached for the Sun. The Oak trees and all of the Mountain were cared for day and night. You know which group of villagers Coyote ordered to work at night, and which of the villagers continued to work during the day. Those who were undecided about whether or not to obey Coyote or follow Skunk work sometimes at night and sometimes in the day. Thus, you can see Deer and Mountain Lion going about at any time. And don't worry about the Cave. Coyote commanded Skunk to make sure the white rock is always rolled back so that the Cave can see her daughter passing by with her handsome suitor. Poor Skunk, he still has that white stripe, and if he gets excited and lifts his tail the tiny satchel opens and lets out that terrible smell—which is why to this day no one follows Skunk.

Part 10

*A*nswer Woman finished telling the story about how Skunk unleashed the Night, and then she was quiet. By this time, the sun, now a red ball, was sinking further and further below the horizon. Already, the western star shone in the distance. Only a few honking geese flying in a line were left in the sky. The other birds had found their roosts. The air had become chilly. The tops of the oak trees were bare; already leaves lay in thick piles on the ground. Certainly autumn was upon the Mountain, and before long winter and cold would indeed arrive.

Question Woman, sitting alongside her twin sister, finally broke the silence. "Okay," she said, "I understand how we got Night on this Mountain, but I still don't know why we have to have winter and cold. You said, 'Everything changes,' and that we need change to see and feel, to know we are alive. Wouldn't it be enough just to have Night and Day? Wouldn't that be enough to see difference in the world? Why do we have to have the seasons, especially winter, when it is wet and cold?"

"Dear Sister, how else are the grasses going to grow? When will the flowers know to bloom? How will Quail know when to lay her eggs?"

"Hey, I'm the one who is supposed to ask the questions!"

"Ah, you are right. But answers come from questions—and

sometimes questions are themselves the answers."

"Okay," said Question Woman, "but I still want an answer to my first question. I want to know why we *have to have* the seasons. Couldn't grasses grow anytime? Couldn't flowers bloom anytime? Couldn't Quail lay her eggs whenever she felt like it?"

"Oh, I see what you are asking," answered Answer Woman. "Well, let me say first that it isn't enough just to see and feel change. We must know when to change too. We must change with the changes. That is the very secret of all life. Anyone or anything that doesn't change will dry up and die. This magical Mountain with all of its moving life will pass us by."

"So don't get left behind."

"Yes, that's right."

"But still, Sister, why do we have to have seasons to know this?"

"I'll tell you," Answer Woman said. "We have to have a time to live our lives and a time to think about them. Remember, stories are the only things we have to help us think about our lives. Change is not just about seeing and feeling the differences. Change also gives us the opportunity to learn from the differences and to think. Change then gives us the opportunity to make our lives better. Again, all of life learns and changes. Each spring the grasses grow and the flowers bloom, but you will see, if you look closely, that they have changed. Maybe there is more grass, maybe less. Each spring a quail will build her nest a little differently, or in a different place altogether. Everything has learned to change in order to live well. Winter is the time to tell stories, to talk about what we have learned, so that, if we need to, we can change what we do when spring comes again. That way we come back new and beautiful like all of life on this Mountain. Winter is a gift. It is the time we have to sit by the fire, when all the harvesting and gathering is finished, so that we can tell stories."

"You've convinced me, Sister. So now tell me, how did we get the seasons?"

"That of course is a story. Listen."

The Bat Brothers Banish Warm Wind

*T*his too happened when the animals were still people. At that time there were seven brothers in the village and each one of them was looking for a wife. These seven bachelors were bats and they lived in a large house wherein each one of them had his own room. Each brother was equally hardworking and handsome.

"Our father has moved to another house and left this large house to us so that we can marry and bring our brides to live here," said the oldest brother. "We must now find wives."

The oldest brother was the leader, especially now that the father was gone, and each of the younger brothers did what the older brother said to do.

"We must go to the old men of the village and ask their advice about choosing a wife," the older brother said.

Straight away the seven Bat Brothers went to see the wise old men.

"Ah, you boys are in a bit of a predicament," said Yellow Jacket, one of the old men. "You must choose women that will get along with one another because they will all be living in the same house as you. Isn't that right?"

"Yes," said the oldest brother. "So what must we look for? How can we tell if the wives will get along with one another?"

The seven brothers were seated around the fire with the old

men. Besides Yellow Jacket, there was also Flea, Blue Jay, and Bear, all old men there to advise the brothers.

"Well," said Yellow Jacket, scratching his chin, "I can tell you this. None of the wives can be jealous, the kind of person who would be envious and say or do mean things to one of the other wives."

Flea then looked up from the fire and spoke. "None of the wives can be unfriendly, the kind of person who would not be warm and kind to each and every one of the other wives."

Then Blue Jay said, "And none of the wives can be too loud or talkative, the kind of person who would be rude and not listen when each of the other wives had something to say."

And then Bear said, "None of the wives can be lazy, the kind of person who wouldn't pitch in and do her share of the work."

Then another old man came along and joined the circle. He was Badger, and he said he had some very important advice to contribute. "You must consider the mothers of each of your potential wives," he said. "You must make sure the mothers possess the same qualities as their daughters, for it is very important that the daughters' mothers get along with everyone also. And, above all else, always respect the mothers."

"Well, that is good advice. Thank you," said the oldest Bat Brother. "You are wise and good old men. Now my brothers and I must set out to find wives."

Before long the seven Bat Brothers discovered that finding seven women who could all live in the same house and get along was not that easy. The oldest brother courted Titmouse, and she told him, "I do not want to share my house with six other women." Another brother courted Sparrow Hawk, and she told him, "No, I don't want to cook food all day just so a bunch of people besides my husband can eat it." And another brother courted Blue Bird, and she said, "No, I don't want to have to listen to other people talking in my house, not when I'm married." And a fourth brother courted Black Beetle and she told him, "No, I don't want to clean and wash clothes for other women, not in my house, not when I'm married." Two of the remaining brothers found no potential wives at all. And the seventh brother courted Mallard Duck, who, as it turned out, was kind and friendly, but whose mother, Goose Woman, was loud and ornery.

"Now what are we going to do?" lamented the oldest brother. "We can't even find one potential wife with all of the qualities the wise old men spoke of. Now we must go back and ask the wise old men if there is anything they can do to help us in our quest."

On their way back to the fire circle where the old men sat, the seven Bat Brothers came upon Turtle, a wise old woman.

"Why the sad look on your faces?" she asked the brothers.

"We cannot find wives," answered the oldest brother, at which point Turtle began to laugh.

"I don't believe that," she said. "Each of you is hardworking and handsome."

"Well, maybe so," answered the oldest Bat Brother, "but

you tell us where we can find seven wonderful women who will be able to live in the same house and get along with one another."

"Ah, I forgot. You boys don't have the best eyes. You don't see very well, particularly during the day when the Sun is bright. You haven't looked far, have you?"

"We have looked everywhere in the village for seven good wives," the oldest brother assured Turtle.

"Yes, my point exactly," said Turtle. "Below the Mountain in a small meadow lives a kind and good woman with seven beautiful daughters, each of whom is as warm and generous as the next. Have you forgotten all about Warm Wind and her seven daughters?"

"How could we have forgotten them?" cried the oldest brother in disbelief. "Brothers, we must go there right now!"

"Oh, but wait a minute," said Turtle. "I must tell you a little something about Warm Wind."

"Well then, what is it?" said the oldest brother, nonetheless anxious to make his way down the Mountain to where Warm Wind and her daughters lived.

Turtle blinked her shiny eyes, then said, "Warm Wind was once married to Mole. Mole is the father of the seven sisters. But Mole proved to be a rather untrustworthy and disloyal husband. So, after a while, Warm Wind left Mole and raised the seven daughters by herself. Now she is getting older and the daughters take good care of her. Indeed, the daughters are good women. Without them Warm Wind would not be able to make her trip back and forth to the large eastern valley, where she goes every year to visit her brothers and sisters. Her father is the Sun, which is why when she is below the Mountain we feel her warmth. In any event, what I am telling you is that you must prove that you will be trustworthy and loyal husbands to Warm Wind's daughters and you must be ever respectful to her."

"Yes," said the oldest Bat Brother as he and the others turned to rush down the Mountain.

There in the small meadow the Bat Brothers found Warm Wind and her seven daughters. They were seated under an oak tree, and the little house where they lived was behind them, just a short distance from the tree. Everywhere in the meadow, flowers blossomed and it was warm. The brothers fell immediately in love, each young bachelor with his eyes fixed on the bride he hoped for. And as Turtle had reminded the brothers, each of the sisters was as beautiful and kind-hearted as the next. Warm Wind sat in the middle of the circle weaving a beautiful basket while her seven daughters kept busy stitching and mending clothes. The Bat Brothers became totally enchanted as Warm Wind and the seven sisters, seemingly oblivious to the suitors, continued to work, singing the most beautiful songs. Warm Wind sang thus:

> *Daughters, daughters*
>
> *A basket of woodpecker feathers*
>
> *I am weaving*

Red woodpecker feathers

The color of the Sun

and when she finished, her daughters followed with their song:

Mother, dear Mother

Garments made of poppy petals

We are sewing

Golden poppy petals

The color of the Sun

Back and forth Warm Wind and her seven daughters continued singing. When the brothers looked again, they found in Warm Wind's hands a round basket made of red feathers from a woodpecker's head. In each of the daughters' hands was a flowing gown made from golden poppy petals. The brothers could not believe their eyes. They had never seen such a sight so lovely, nor heard such lovely songs.

"I can't believe we didn't think of these girls before," said the oldest Bat Brother.

"But how do we get their attention?" asked the youngest brother. "We could stand here all day and still they would not look up from their work."

Then, as if the sisters had been listening all along, they looked up and found the handsome brothers.

"We are in love and wish to marry you," announced the oldest Bat Brother.

The sisters, sitting very still, did not respond.

Then the youngest Bat Brother remembered something very important about courting: Every maiden has a special song that she will teach the man she picks to be her husband. The man must learn to sing that special song, and only that way can he become her true husband.

"Brother," the youngest Bat Brother said, "we must follow the ancient courting rule. Maybe that way these girls will talk to us."

Thus reminded of the courting rule, the oldest brother said to the sisters, "If you would so honor us, would you teach us your special song in order that we might answer your song and be your true husbands?"

The sisters indeed found the Bat Brothers handsome and knew that the brothers were hardworking, each and every one. The oldest sister spoke, telling the brothers as much, and the brothers were overcome with joy. "But still," the oldest sister said, "we would not think of marrying without our mother's permission."

"And don't forget that our mother is getting old," the youngest sister said. "Our grandfather, the Sun, can show her the way back and forth to the eastern valley each year, but we must accompany her, for the journey is long and she will get tired."

All the while, the old mother, Warm Wind, continued working

on her basket. When at last she set the basket down, she looked at her daughters and then at their anxious suitors.

"Well," she said, looking back at her daughters, "your father, Mole, once courted me and I gave him my special song, but in the end he proved untrustworthy and disloyal. I am doubtful of men's intentions...But my experience must not prejudice my daughters' thinking. Certainly my lovely daughters must think for themselves and make their own decisions. I have raised them well."

The Bat Brothers were relieved, for they had thought that perhaps Warm Wind was not going to give her daughters permission to marry. But then the youngest daughter spoke and the brothers became worried once again.

"Dear Mother," she said, "I must remind you that you are getting old. How will you get plenty to eat every day? And if you were to walk back and forth every year to visit your brothers and sisters in the big eastern valley, you would be forever walking. With help you get back and forth in a week; without our help you would be walking the entire year—even if your father, the Sun, was guiding you."

"Now listen, Daughter, don't worry about me. I can still cook and clean for myself. I can gather clover and acorns and haul wood for a fire. And once a year you girls can help me back and forth to the big eastern valley to visit my brothers and sisters. Please, don't worry. You are all women now. You must live your lives. I raised you well."

The anxious brothers were once again relieved, and then to

their amazement and great satisfaction they heard the seven sisters begin singing thus:

> *Alongside Warm Wind*
>
> *Wedding garments made of poppy petals*
>
> *I am seeing*
>
> *Golden poppy petals*
>
> *The color of the Sun*

And that way, singing the beautiful sisters' special song, the seven Bat Brothers led the seven sisters back up the Mountain to their big house in the village and married the sisters there. The brothers found that old woman Turtle had been completely correct: Each sister was as lovely as the next. They worked hard and got along with each other wonderfully, even as the big house became more and more crowded with children, for as it turned out each sister had many children. Before long there were so many children in the house that they could not be counted. Still, these wonderful daughters of Warm Wind managed to keep a peaceful and happy home together.

Each year the daughters kept their promise to Warm Wind and accompanied her to visit her brothers and sisters. They were gone from the big house and the village for about a week. They followed the Sun, Warm Wind's father; and, helping their mother, the journey only took them three days each way. Warm Wind never stayed too long. She was happy to visit for one day and see that her beloved brothers and sisters were doing well. During the time she was gone, the village was cold, for there was little warmth coming up the Mountain from Warm Wind's meadow. The light too was very dull, for the Sun was away, busy leading his daughter and granddaughters to the big eastern valley.

Then, as it turned out, one of Warm Wind's brothers died, and the family asked if she could stay an extra day in order to attend the funeral with them. Her daughters assured her that it was absolutely fine that she stay for their uncle's funeral. "What is an extra day to our good and hardworking husbands?" they said.

When the seven sisters at last returned to the big house, they found the Bat Brothers had done a fine job taking care of the many children. The sisters were happy to see their husbands and their children. But about a week after they had returned, the oldest sister and the youngest sister went to check on Warm Wind and found she was not in her little house by the oak trees.

"Where is our mother?" they asked.

They searched the meadow and nowhere could she be found. And they became quite worried, for the air was cold and the flowers were no longer blooming. The leaves on the trees were turning colors and falling to the ground.

"Something has happened to our mother," the youngest sister said.

They were extremely worried now. They noticed also that the light was dull. They could not see their grandfather, the Sun, at his usual place on top of the Mountain.

"Something terrible has happened," said the youngest sister again.

"Now, don't worry," said the oldest sister. "Perhaps grandfather Sun has taken Mother for a walk someplace and soon they will return."

But, unfortunately, that was not what had happened. It was something far worse, and, of all people, it was Mole, their father, who stepped forth to help them. He told them something awful. He said that their husbands had captured their beloved mother and locked her in a cave. Mole claimed that the Bat Brothers had been getting more and more upset about their wives leaving for a week. He said the brothers were complaining that, with more children in the house each year, they had more work to do when their wives were gone. The brothers squabbled with one another about taking turns cleaning and cooking for all those children. They found that getting along with one another was hard work. When the sisters stayed an extra day this last time for their uncle's funeral, the brothers decided to do something about the wives' trips once and for all. They decided to kidnap Warm Wind and hide her in a cave where she would eventually starve to death and die. The brothers then went after the Sun to tie him to the top of the Mountain so he could never move away either, but, said Mole, the Sun escaped and ran far south.

The two sisters could not believe what they were hearing.

"You were an untrustworthy husband and Mother had to raise us by herself," said the oldest sister. "Why should we believe you? What have you ever done for us?"

"You are the one who took Mother!" accused the youngest sister. "You're the one who took her, not our beloved bat husbands."

"No," said Mole. "I was here, close to your mother's house. I heard what your husbands were saying. I heard them plotting and planning to kidnap your mother. I could not get to her in time to help her, but I know where she is. If you follow me, I will take you to the cave."

Neither of the two sisters trusted their father. But, thinking of their mother, they followed him to a cave near the foot of the Mountain. The cave was small and the sisters quickly discovered that their mother was not there. But on the floor they found ropes and ties made from, of all things, their wedding gowns.

"What happened?" cried the sisters. "Where is our mother?"

Mole was crying now too, for he did not know what had happened to Warm Wind and he feared the worst. "If I couldn't help her, I can still help you," he said. "Please run, go home, for tonight, just after midnight, your husbands are going to lock you in their big house forever. Right now they are busy making the ropes to tie you with. On your way home, you will see them. They are behind two large rocks just this side of the village. Watch them, but get home safely and warn your sisters."

The sisters, who still did not totally trust Mole, nonetheless ran off. But when they found all seven husbands behind the two large rocks, just as Mole had said, they no longer doubted him. The Bat Brothers were busying making rope from the torn and shredded golden poppy wedding gowns.

When the two sisters got back to the big house, they told the other disbelieving sisters what had happened. They showed them the rope, made of their wedding gowns, that had been used to tie their mother.

"What happened to our mother?" the middle sisters cried. "How will we ever find her?"

That was when the oldest sister told the others her plan. "We must escape," she said. "We must leave before our husbands return at midnight, and we must take our children with us."

"But where can we escape to?" asked the youngest sister. "There are seven of them and surely one will find us. The Mountain is not that large."

"We will go to the sky and live there," the oldest sister answered.

Which was what happened. Just before midnight the oldest sister led her sisters and all of the children into the sky. There they were safe. They looked down and found their grandfather, the Sun, in the south. They could not find their mother, but they heard her singing in the eastern valley:

I have left my basket made of woodpecker feathers

My brothers and sisters have a part of me

Never mind no one sees me

I am free

I move back and forth to my house in the meadow

Never mind I travel slowly

I am safe

Following my father as he goes

I move back and forth to my house in the meadow

Never mind I am alone

I am happy

Seeing my children at night in the sky

That is how the seven sisters became the Big Dipper and how their many children became the many other stars, and the grandchildren and great-grandchildren became the stars of the Milky Way. And that is how we got the four long seasons: winter, spring, summer, and fall, instead of just one cold winter week each year as before. Warm Wind moves slowly, following the Sun as he moves north to south and then back again each year.

As for the Bat Brothers, they remain forever lost and confused, looking for their wives and children. They fly around all night without looking up. And during the day, they hang upside down looking up when their wives and children are not in the sky. As for Mole, he redeemed himself and garnered Warm Wind's affections once more. They are both old now, but come spring and summer when Warm Wind is in the meadow, they often visit and at night look up at their many children and grandchildren.

Part 11

By the time Answer Woman finished telling Question Woman the story about the Bat Brothers, the sky above Sonoma Mountain had grown dark. Night had befallen the land. Twinkling stars filled the sky, and straight overhead shone a milky quarter moon.

"It is long past the time when we should have started for home," remarked Answer Woman.

"Well, that last story you told us was a long one," said Question Woman.

The twin sisters were still perched atop the fence on Gravity Hill, their usual spot; and indeed, it was late and they had yet to journey up the Mountain to where they slept safely tucked amidst the branches of an ancient bay laurel tree.

"C'mon, let's go," said Answer Woman. "It is freezing cold and I want to go home for the night."

She saw that her sister was peering up at the sky, looking at the numerous twinkling stars and moon.

"What are you doing, Question Woman?" she asked. "Come on, let's go. It has become so cold that the stars feel like icicles hanging up there."

"But, Sister, that's what I am thinking about right now—feeling the cold, cold night is not at all pleasant. Why does the cold have to hurt? Can't we have wet and cold so that it doesn't ever hurt us? Why must we have pain?"

"Oh my goodness, those are big questions," said Answer Woman.

"Please, before we go home for the night, give me the answer," pleaded Question Woman.

"Well, all right, but listen carefully...To feel wet and cold is one thing. It lets us know to change, as I told you before. But only the threat of pain—only knowing that the wet and cold can hurt—provides any guarantee that we will change. The possibility of pain, of getting hurt, is a condition of living on this Mountain. That is how we keep our promise to the Mountain to behave. If we don't behave, if we don't learn and live well, we could get hurt somehow. If there was no way to get hurt, we would forget the rules and lessons of this Mountain and then maybe would hurt other people and other parts of this glorious place. Pain, or the threat of pain, keeps us humble. We are reminded to think of others and learn all of the lessons the stories have to teach us."

"So how did pain get into things? How did pain come about?"

"Now you've asked the big question," said Answer Woman. "We'll be here all night."

"Please, tell me the story."

"All right. Listen carefully. It's the story of how a mountain was made."

Ant Uncovers a Plot

*A*t that time the land was flat. There were no hills or mountains. The animal people were living at the same place in a village near the headwaters of Copeland Creek; but the village was not yet atop the great Mountain, and the creek ran straight along the wide open plain to the sea. At that time there lived a very noble woman in the village whom the people called Eagle. She had adopted her orphan nephew, Kite, a thin, pale boy with long straight arms. Eagle loved the boy and did an excellent job providing for him and teaching him the important lessons that would help him be a good citizen of the village. Eagle was herself a very hard worker, going near and far to gather acorns and seeds. Also, she was a skillful tree climber; and, even though the entire world was flat and people could see far into the distance, it was useful to gaze from the height of a tall tree in order to see where exactly seeds were ripening or where fresh blackberries grew on a clump of vines.

Then one morning Kite noticed that Eagle looked troubled.

"Aunt, you don't seem to be yourself," said Kite. "What seems to be the problem?"

"Nephew," Eagle answered, "last night I dreamed that I was falling out of a tall oak tree. Today I am afraid to climb trees and scout for the acorns you and the other villagers need."

"Oh, Aunt, it was just a dream. Do not be afraid," said Kite.

But, as it turned out, Eagle continued to have this bad dream every night. She dreamed that just as she was reaching the top of the tall oak tree, the branches gave way, and she found herself falling helplessly to the ground. Soon, she was not only afraid to climb trees but she was afraid even to leave the house. My poor aunt, Kite thought to himself. She has been so good to me, feeding and caring for me, and now I must do something to help her.

In those days, if a person had bad dreams and became frightened, that person, or one of his or her relatives, would go to the village's doctors. There were four doctors and these doctors always worked together. There was not yet any pain in the world. Bad dreams and frightening thoughts were the only illnesses then, and these four doctors knew just what to do to make a person happy again. The first doctor, a very big man, boiled herbs that helped the patient relax. The second doctor, a very talkative man, told stories that made the patient think good thoughts. The third doctor, a short man, tended the fire to keep the healing house warm. And the fourth doctor, a very tall man, sang songs that would keep bad dreams and thoughts from returning to the patient.

Kite thought immediately of the four doctors, and he went and told them of his aunt's bad dream. "My good aunt dreams every night that she is falling out of a tall oak tree," Kite said. "No longer will she even leave the house, much less scout for acorns and blackberries." The doctors told Kite to bring his aunt to them, whereupon Kite went home and found Eagle and returned with her to the healing house.

In the healing house Eagle lay on a soft bed of goose down by the fire. The first doctor, the very big man, boiled herbs and sang thus:

The down feathers hold you

Touching soft, soft, soft

And the walls of the healing house are strong

The second doctor, the very talkative man, told a story and then sang thus:

The story fills your eyes

Healthy villagers dancing, dancing, dancing

And the roof of the healing house is strong

Then the third doctor, the short man, tossed a manzanita branch into the fire and sang thus:

The sun has found you

The first day of summer walking closer, closer, closer

And the floor of the healing house holds

And then the fourth doctor, the very tall man, sang a song and then finished with this song:

The melody plants itself in you

A strong seed sprouting, sprouting, sprouting

And the door of the healing house is forever secure

The doctors worked on Eagle at night. During the day, while Eagle slept soundly in the healing house, the doctors collected along the creek. They bathed in the water and then discussed the patient amongst themselves, which was their custom.

"How do you think Eagle will do?" asked the very big herb doctor.

"Oh, she will be fine," answered the talkative story doctor.

"She has had a very bad dream, so bad that she can no longer scout for the village," said the short fire doctor, "but I do believe also that she will do just fine."

"Yes," chimed in the very tall singing doctor, "I will sing my songs especially loudly for her."

"Well," said the very big herb doctor, "you both have just reminded me of what I was thinking earlier while I was taking a bath."

"And what is that?" asked the tall singing doctor.

"Well, you just said it yourself. Look at how loud you must sing for Eagle. And you, Story Doctor, look what a long story you must tell Eagle every night. And you, Fire Doctor, you must use manzanita, the best wood to heat the healing house for Eagle."

"I still don't see your point," said the tall singing doctor. "What are you thinking?"

"I am thinking how it is not fair that all patients, no matter how rich or poor, pay us the same amount, which is a single clamshell disc bead. Why, at the rate we collect disc beads, we hardly have enough beads for a single necklace every five years. Look at Eagle: People offer her many beads anytime she tells them where she has seen a good cache of acorns from her treetop. She owns enough beads for twenty necklaces. We are healing her so she can return to her scouting business and climb trees, whereupon people will just give her more and more beads."

"But Eagle does not ask for any payment from people," said the short fire doctor. "And she is doing something to help feed all of the village."

"And let us not forget that Eagle uses whatever payment she gets to help her raise her nephew, Kite," said the talkative story doctor.

"And what's left over she gives to other people and needy children," added the tall singing doctor.

"I'm not saying we should steal all of her beads," said the big herb doctor.

"What are you saying then?" asked the tall singing doctor.

"Look, you guys said it yourself: Eagle does something to help the village, and people reward her with lots of beads. We are helping Eagle so that she can continue to help the village and we will get only one bead. Is there any reason *we* shouldn't get *just a few more* beads for healing Eagle then?"

None of the three other doctors was able to think of an answer, and right then the big herb doctor revealed to them his plan to get more beads from Eagle. "We will keep her sick for a while. That way her nephew will feel obliged to bring us more than one bead for helping his aunt."

"No, that is not a good idea," said the talkative story doctor. "I don't want to do anything like that to Eagle."

"I don't want to do anything harmful to Eagle either," said the short fire doctor.

"Me either," said the tall singing doctor.

"Who said anything about hurting Eagle?" said the big herb doctor. "She will simply sleep longer. And none of you have to do anything. I will give her a potion that will make her sleep. All you have to do is keep quiet."

The three doctors thought awhile and then agreed to the plan, but only on the condition that Eagle was not harmed in any way and that Eagle did not have to keep sleeping for too long.

Usually the doctors treated a patient four nights in the healing house, and on the morning after the last night of treatment the patient's closest friend or relative went with a single clamshell disc bead to pay the doctors for their services and to bring the patient home. Following this custom, Kite went with a single clamshell disc bead to the healing house on the morning after Eagle's fourth night of treatment. But, to his surprise, he found only the very big herb doctor at the door of the healing house and none of the other doctors—and, most surprising of all, not his aunt, Eagle.

Offering the disc bead in his upturned hand, he said to the big herb doctor, "I've come to take my good aunt home," at which point the big herb doctor explained that Eagle had experienced a particularly harmful dream and that she would have to stay in the healing house at least another week.

When a week had passed, Kite returned to the healing house. But, alas, he was told by the big herb doctor that his aunt would have to stay in the healing house yet another week. Then, when Kite went back the third time, he was told the same thing—that his aunt would have to stay in the healing house yet one more week.

"Look," said the big herb doctor to the other doctors sitting at the back of the healing house. "We now have three clamshell disc beads."

The three other doctors did not say anything in return, and they had gloomy looks on their faces.

"Why the gloomy faces?" asked the big herb doctor. He pointed to Eagle on the down bed with a rabbit skin blanket draped over her body. "Look, Eagle is sleeping and we have had to do nothing the last two weeks to earn two extra beads."

The short fire doctor spoke up, saying, "Already I think Eagle has been sleeping too long. I think it is time to let her go."

The two others, the talkative story doctor and the tall singing doctor, agreed. They reminded the big herb doctor that they had agreed to this scheme only on the condition that Eagle was not harmed and did not have to sleep for too long.

"How does Eagle know how much time has passed?" asked the big herb doctor. "She has been sleeping peacefully this whole time."

As it turned out, Kite went back week after week to fetch his aunt home, only to hand the big herb doctor another disc bead and be told to come back again the following week. An entire year passed. Kite trusted the doctors, but he missed his aunt greatly. Often he would sit on a rock and cry. The rock was a good distance from the village, for he did not want the villagers to catch him crying. It was his beloved aunt, after all, who had told him always to be brave, and he didn't want to disappoint the woman who had set such a good example for him.

But one person did catch him crying. It was Ant, who was out gathering seeds when he found the boy hunched over on the rock, crying.

"Ah, why the sadness, young man?" asked Ant.

Ant was a small man who was always jolly. He was a trusted friend to many people in the village, for he often gave people good advice—which must have been the reason Kite confessed how sad he was and how much he missed his aunt. "I have not seen my aunt for over a year."

Kite told Ant the entire story about Eagle and the bad dream of falling out of a tall oak tree. Ant grew suspicious when he heard that Eagle had been in the healing house an entire year. He did not convey his concerns to Kite but told him only not to worry, that certainly Eagle would get well and come home soon.

Ant went off then and began thinking. It occurred to him that over the past year he had many times come upon the big herb doctor digging up soaproot bulbs on the other side of Copeland Creek, out of sight from the village. People used soaproot bulbs to wash their hair. Soaproot bulb, when mashed up, was also used to make fish fall asleep in the water so that fishermen could catch the fish easily. Well, the big herb doctor certainly can't be washing his hair that much, thought Ant.

Ant grew more and more suspicious, wondering how Eagle could possibly spend an entire year inside the healing house. One day he went to the place across the creek where he'd seen the big herb doctor digging soaproot bulbs. He hid inside the hairy bark of a bulb. At last the big herb doctor dug up the bulb and carried it in a basket back to the healing house. And so, hidden within the hairy bark of a soaproot bulb, Ant got inside the healing house. When the big herb doctor set the basket down, Ant jumped out from behind the hairy bark and hid safely in a stack of wood in the corner of the room. From there Ant watched as the big herb doctor mashed the bulbs and made a potion, mixing them with warm water. Then, just as Ant suspected, he saw the big herb doctor wake Eagle just long enough to give her more of the potion, while the three other doctors sat idly by at the back of the room. Then, when night came and all four doctors were asleep, Ant escaped.

He went to Coyote, the headman of the village, and told him everything he had seen. "Why, the soaproot bulb concoction is not just putting Eagle to sleep, it is poisoning her. She has not eaten anything else for a year and soon she will die," said Ant.

Coyote was greatly alarmed. Even though it was the middle of the night, he summoned the strongest men and women of the village and instructed them to arrest the four doctors and set poor Eagle free. A posse of strong men and women went to the healing house and returned to Coyote with the four doctors.

"You were supposed to heal people, not poison them," said an angry Coyote to the doctors.

"I only wanted a few more clamshell disc beads," said the big herb doctor. "I didn't mean to hurt anyone."

"The gift of healing is a great reward in and of itself," answered Coyote, who felt no sympathy for the big herb doctor or any of the other three guilty doctors. "All of you must be punished," he said.

At that point, Coyote consulted with his wise nephew Chicken Hawk. Then Coyote told the doctors what he was going to do with them. "You must be separated, since you can't be trusted to work together in the healing house ever again," he said. He told the three doctors who went along with the big herb doctor's scheme that they were just as guilty as the big herb doctor on account of the fact that they knew what was going on and did nothing to help Eagle.

"You will each become mountains," Coyote said.

He sent the tall singing doctor far north. "You will be Mount Saint Helena, and you will forever provide the people with songs."

He sent the short fire doctor north also, but not nearly as far. "You will be Mount Taylor, and you will forever provide the people with wood for fires."

He looked then at the talkative story doctor. "You will stay right here and be Sonoma Mountain, and you will forever provide the people with stories so that they will be reminded not to make the mistakes you and the other doctors have made."

Then he looked long and hard at the big herb doctor. "You were the ringleader. You must go far south the sit near the ocean and forever protect the people from cold storms. You will be Mount Tamalpais, and much soaproot and other poisonous herbs will grow upon you, and the people therefore will forever know to suspect any man or woman who dares to visit you. People should pick the good herbs that grow at your feet and not go high up upon you."

And, that way, having been given their sentences, they were marched to the places where each of them would stay from that night on.

Meanwhile, Ant found Kite, and together they waited inside the healing house for Eagle to wake. Close to morning, they were startled when Eagle woke all at once and began screaming hysterically. "My legs, my legs!" Eagle hollered, wild-eyed.

Attempting to see what was the matter, Ant lifted the rabbit skin blanket from Eagle. Kite and Ant nearly fainted at the sight of what they found. The big herb doctor had bound Eagle's legs tightly with rope. The bottom part of Eagle's legs, below the rope, had long ago fallen off. And now, after a year, the top of her legs were yellow-colored and full of infection.

Hearing the screaming, the villagers raced into the healing house. They had never heard such terrible screaming before. To their amazement, they found Eagle now flopping all over the floor, pushing and struggling as if to get away from the infected stubs that were all that was left of her legs.

"What is happening?" a frightened woman in the congregation cried.

"Somebody, please help my aunt!" cried Kite.

Eagle continued writhing and flopping uncontrollably on the ground, pushing and struggling, screaming at the top of her lungs.

Ant saw that Eagle's stubs were raw and ugly with the infection. Without thinking, only wanting to help Eagle, Ant found two four-pronged digging sticks and quickly shoved them into Eagle's stubs to stop the festering.

Eagle calmed down a bit, and then the confused villagers began to talk amongst themselves. They wondered what had happened, for they had never seen anyone acting this way. Then, they noticed that Eagle had begun to rise into the air. She was propelling herself higher and higher, using her arms, which had grown immense and powerful from all of her struggling on the ground. And she was singing to her bewildered nephew thus:

Into the heavens we go

You and me

I am taking you

Taking you forever with me

Hey-hey hey-hey

Soaring in the heavens

You and me

I am taking you

Taking you forever home

Hey-hey hey-hey

And, singing that song, Eagle flew out of the healing house. And Kite, her adoring nephew, was right behind her, for with the help of Eagle's song and powerful heart Kite too grew wings.

The villagers went out then and found it was morning. And, lo and behold, they were atop a tall Mountain. They could see the Santa Rosa Plain below and clear to the ocean. And they could see Mount Tamalpais in the south and, just north, Mount Taylor, and yet further north, Mount Saint Helena. The villagers knew then that they were atop Sonoma Mountain, where they would live until the end of time. But they still wondered about what they had seen with the strange and frightening behavior displayed by Eagle in the healing house. Again, they began to talk amongst themselves.

Chicken Hawk knew what had happened, and he quietly told Coyote. They wondered if they should tell the villagers, for the world would never be the same again, and they didn't want to frighten the villagers with the news.

"You must tell us," Ant said.

"Yes, you are right," Coyote said to Ant. "You uncovered the secret the four doctors were keeping, and there should never be any such secrets again."

Then Coyote stepped forward and told the villagers what he knew:

"What you saw last night in the healing house was *Pain*. What Eagle suffered was Pain. Pain is now loose amongst us. Eagle's infection spread in the air. It is set loose. From now on we will feel it, each and every one of us, at one time or another in our lives. Maybe our heads will hurt, maybe the joints in our legs and arms. But fear not, the four doctors have not left us. They have learned their lesson well and yearn each and every day to be of service to us. Mount Saint Helena will forever give us songs, and Mount Taylor wood for fires. This wondrous Mountain where we now live will forever be telling us stories. And as long as we stick to the bottom of Mount Tamalpais, we will be supplied with fine herbs. Yes, the songs, the good wood, the stories, and the herbs from the mountains will cure us and keep us well and safe. But we cannot forget Pain and the lesson to be learned from it."

When Coyote finished talking, he looked up into the sky. The villagers then did the same. There was Eagle soaring high above the Mountain and, just below her, her beloved nephew Kite. Everyone knew then what Coyote said was true. At the same time, seeing Eagle flying high above them, higher even than the tallest mountain, they knew that in Eagle they had the greatest protector ever to watch over them, for she was singing thus:

Seeing Forever

My eyes, my eyes

I offer you

Seeing Truth

My eyes, my eyes

I offer you

Seeing Lies

My eyes, my eyes

I offer you

Seeing Forever

This song, this song

I sing for you

The people felt better and began to disperse. But, once more, Coyote stopped them. He was holding the bag that the big herb doctor had used to hide all the clamshell disc beads he had taken each week from Eagle's trusting nephew, Kite. He handed each person in the congregation a disc bead.

"But these disc beads really belong to Eagle," Ant said.

Coyote laughed and tossed his bead into the air. Then Ant and everyone else tossed their beads into the air like Coyote. All at once, the beads became prisms of light, and these words fell from the sky:

> *Seeing Forever*
>
> *My eyes, my eyes*
>
> *I offer you*

> *Seeing Truth*
>
> *My eyes, my eyes*
>
> *I offer you*

> *Seeing Lies*
>
> *My eyes, my eyes*
>
> *I offer you*

Seeing Forever

This song, this song

I sing for you.

Part 12

*O*ne day that same season, as Question Woman and Answer Woman sat atop the fence on Gravity Hill, clouds gathered in the sky. A slight wind blew, and the top of Sonoma Mountain was hidden behind the thick gray-black clouds. Even the sprawling valley below the Mountain was dark without any bright light from the sun.

"It is going to rain," remarked Answer Woman. "We should find cover just as the other birds and animals have done."

Question Woman, the twin sister, glanced about the hillsides and found no animals, no rabbits feeding on clover along the road, not a single deer grazing further on in the meadows. The trees were silent; birds didn't flit and sing amidst the branches.

"You are right as always," said Question Woman to her sister. "But, tell me, why does it have to rain? Isn't it enough that at this time of year the days grow short and the nights become very cold?" Then, before her sister could answer, Question Woman continued thus: "I know water makes the plants grow. But why couldn't the plants find a way to grow without them? When it rains everything on the Mountain gets wet. Things get messy when it rains—there's mud. And all of us have to run for cover and then sit and wait until the rain goes away. I don't want it to rain!"

"Ah, dear Sister," said Answer Woman. "Don't speak like that. Rain feeds all plants; it feeds all of life. But it also reminds us of an important story. After all, Rain is the keeper of all memories, and without memories we would not be able to remember a thing—nothing would stick in our brains."

"You mean everyone would be like me, unable to remember a thing?" said Question Woman.

"Worse," answered Answer Woman. "You wouldn't even know to ask questions. If there were no memories, there would be nothing that you forgot. There would be no answers."

"I see."

"So, listen. Without memories we would not remember the stories. And without memories of the stories, we would forget how to live and then quickly die—just like all of life without rain."

"I think I understand. But why is Rain the keeper of memories? Why not something else that all of us need, like the sun or the air?"

"Well, that's the story."

"Tell it, please."

"Now, when it is about to rain?"

"Please."

"Well, then listen."

Rain Finds a Home in the Sky

*I*n that ancient village on Copeland Creek, near the top of this wondrous Mountain, there lived a beautiful woman called Rain. Many people considered Rain the most important person in the village, even more important than the headman Coyote, though Rain, a most humble and kind person, would never have considered herself more important or worthy than anyone else. She was beautiful to gaze upon indeed, for she was tall and went about in billowing gowns made either of white goose down or of gray quail plumage. But her appearance was hardly what others valued most about her. She kept peoples' memories, for in those days long ago, when all of the animals were still people, the villagers did not yet carry around their own memories. Each memory was a stone, a piece of quartz, maybe an obsidian chip, each a different size and shape, that Rain stored in a special basket. She knew whom each of the stones belonged to and for what purpose each was to be used. If a person needed his or her stone—that is, if he or she needed to remember something or to be reminded of something—Rain would fetch the particular stone and let the person hold the stone long enough for the memory to emerge. If, for example, Raccoon needed to remember where to gather berries, Rain would find the stone Raccoon needed. The stone would not only tell Raccoon where to find the berries but also the proper etiquette for gathering them. If Eagle wanted to fish for salmon, there was in Rain's basket a stone that would remind Eagle first to visit Fly, who knew when the salmon would travel upstream as well as the proper songs for fishing the salmon.

Each year the villagers held a basket making contest, and the best basket, selected by a jury of old women, was given to Rain for her memory stones. As it turned out, Mouse, an expert weaver, had won the contest for the last four years. None of the contest baskets was disregarded; all of them were used to line the path to Rain's front door. Thus, each weaver could be proud of his or her work the entire year.

There lived in the village twin Toad Sisters who were also fine weavers. In the past, one or other of the twins had often won the contest.

"What makes Mouse's baskets so special of late?" asked one Toad Sister of the other.

"I don't know," answered the other Toad Sister. "Certainly our baskets have the most beautiful designs. Spider Woman, the greatest basket maker of all, the one who taught all of us to weave, said so herself. She said you and I decorate our baskets with the most beautiful designs. And let us not forget that the jury of judges for the contest always checks with Spider Woman before they make their decision on the winning basket."

"Yes, so what makes Mouse's baskets so beautiful in both the eyes of the judges and old Spider Woman?"

Soon it was time again for the yearly basket making contest.

The contest was held in the fall before the first rains. The jury of old women seated themselves outside of Rain's house, and each of the baskets was tested for its strength as well as judged for its intricate designs. The baskets were expected to hold acorns and seeds without breaking. They were expected to hold water without leaking. Some of the baskets were decorated with feathers, others with colorful beads.

The entire village watched with much anticipation as the judges passed the various beautiful baskets back and forth amongst themselves, studying carefully each basket's quality. On one side of the judges sat old Spider Woman. Even though she was old, her long, bony fingers were agile, and she could still weave the finest baskets of all. Even better were her eyes, for she could detect the slightest flaw in a basket, a missing stitch for instance, or an uneven pattern in the design. Rain looked on also. Earlier that day she had filled each of the previous year's baskets with berries or acorns, some crop from that autumn's harvest, which she would return with the basket to its proud weaver. That was the tradition.

Back and forth the judges passed the baskets. Soon it was evening. The light was waning and the jury would have to make its decision. At long last the old women selected a basket. They gave their selection to Spider Woman for her approval, and after Spider Woman inspected the basket and gave her approval, the old women announced the winner, holding up the beautiful basket for all to see. Once again the winning basket was made by Mouse.

All the while the Toad Sisters had been sitting up front, close to the judges and Spider Woman. They were determined to see what exactly the judges were looking for in a winning basket. Of course they were disappointed when neither of their baskets won the contest. Worse, they could not get an answer to their burning question. They were unable to see what made Mouse's basket so special in the eyes of the judges and Spider Woman.

"We must get our hands on that basket," said one Toad Sister to the other.

"Yes, and when we do, we will take it apart stitch by stitch to see what it is made of," said the other Toad Sister.

The Toad Sisters were both very smart. No wonder then that they came up with a plan to get their hands on Mouse's winning basket, which was now where Rain kept the memory stones. A week later they visited Rain.

"I need to remember where there is a good pond of water to soak my acorns," said one Toad Sister.

"And I need to remember where there is a good pond to dig wild potatoes," said the other Toad Sister.

"Fine," said the lovely Rain, who then went to get her basket of memory stones.

Usually people waited outside while Rain fetched the stones they needed. When Rain answered her door, she found that the twin Toad Sisters had each lugged a heavy sack of acorns to offer as a gift. "Oh, please, come in," the ever grateful Rain said to the Toad Sisters. She offered the sisters tea and acorn bread. But when she went to fetch the memory stones for the twin sisters, they watched to see where she went. To their amazement Mouse's beautiful basket sat on a shelf, out in the open. Rain picked out the two stones that the sisters needed. After the Toad Sisters held their stones long enough to get their answers—where there was a good pond to soak acorns and where there was a good pond to dig wild potatoes—they gave their stones back to Rain and went on their way.

"Why do you suppose Rain keeps Mouse's beautiful basket where anyone can see it?" asked one Toad Sister as they walked home to their house.

"You know the answer to that, Sister. Rain wouldn't imagine that anyone would want to steal the basket. No one would come up with a plan like we have. Why would anyone want that basket except to have everyone's memories, and who on this Mountain would want to be stuck with such a burden?"

Before the Toad Sisters visited Rain, they had gone to see Mouse. They brought a sack of wild potatoes. The grateful Mouse invited the Toad Sisters inside and offered them a slice of warm acorn bread. As they visited together with Mouse, one Sister mentioned that her memory stone for weaving baskets was a sharp little rock with a vein of quartz running through it. Whereupon the unsuspecting Mouse remarked that her memory stone for weaving was nothing near as interesting but was instead a mere round pebble, as plain looking as any pebble one might find in the creek bed.

So, as planned, the Toad Sisters stole into Rain's house one day when she had gone far off into the hills gathering mushrooms. Inside Rain's house, they quickly poured all of the memory stones onto Rain's supper table and then furiously began to take apart Mouse's basket stitch by stitch. They discovered that the inside of the basket had been fortified with short pieces of string. "Ah, we have found Mouse's secret for making the winning basket!" the sisters exclaimed in unison. Thereupon, among the memory stones, they found the plain round pebble Mouse had described. Holding the pebble, the sisters were most surprised, for the pebble began singing thus:

> *At the refuse heap*
>
> *At the refuse heap*
>
> *Even now when there is more than enough*
>
> *I am useful to you*
>
> *I am useful to you*
>
> *I am useful to you*
>
> *Even as the villagers leave pieces behind*
>
> *At the refuse heap*

The Toad Sisters carefully restitched the basket and put all of the memory stones back inside of it and placed it back on Rain's shelf. Then they went home and set about making the most beautiful baskets. That following autumn the villagers witnessed something unique. The jury of old women judges could not decide amongst themselves which of two beautiful and expertly made baskets should win the contest. At last, they gave both baskets to Spider Woman, who, unable to decide herself, declared a tie. The Toad Sisters proudly rose to accept their acclaim from the crowd. Then, following tradition, the previous year's baskets, filled with goods from the harvest, were returned to their makers.

"Who would have thought the secret was old pieces of string left at the garbage heap?" said one Toad Sister to the other on their way home.

"Now we will be able to win the contest every year," said the second Toad Sister.

"Yes," said the first Toad Sister.

But already this first twin Toad had another plan. She did not like the notion of having to share the accolades with her sister year after year. She wanted to win the basket making contest herself. So one day she told her sister that they needed wood for a fire and asked if she wouldn't mind going to the far side of the Mountain to collect some manzanita logs. This was when the first sister noticed Rain leaving the village one morning to visit her friend Fog at the bottom of the Mountain. Her plan was to steal Rain's basket of memory stones—in fact, *both* baskets of memory stones, now that Rain had two winning baskets in which to keep her stones. The first Toad Sister was going to keep the baskets hidden in their house—hidden so that even her sister couldn't find them—long enough to sort through every memory stone and learn every basket maker's secrets. She thought to herself, I will hold each stone long enough to hear it speak or sing. If the memory I hear isn't relevant to basket making, I will put the stone back in its basket. If the memory that emerges concerns basket making, I will uncover with each relevant stone yet another basket making secret.

But this first Toad Sister forgot that her twin was as smart as she was. In fact, just as they looked alike, often they thought alike. The second Toad Sister knew exactly what the first was up to, never mind that she had found where the first Toad Sister had hidden the firewood so that it appeared they had no wood for a fire. When the first Toad Sister returned to the house, the second Toad Sister was waiting for her.

"Listen, sweetie," said the second Toad Sister with a good dose of sarcasm, "I know what you have hidden under your arms."

The first Toad Sister, knowing better, didn't try to fool her sister. She took the two beautiful baskets out from under her arms and set them on the table. "All right," she said, "you caught me."

"This is what we will do," said the second Toad Sister to her guilty sister. "We will each take one basket—the one we made—and that basket will be ours only to sort through the memory stones for basket making secrets."

The guilty sister at this point could do nothing but accept her sister's plan.

"All right, then," said the second sister. "We must first make a fire, since each of our baskets contains so many memory stones and we will have to sit here for some time picking through the stones."

Sheepishly, the first sister found the logs she had hidden under her bed and made a fire. Then, sitting across from one another at the table, the twin Toad Sisters began sorting through the many memory stones in each of their baskets. They had to hold each stone until it sang or spoke a memory. Sometimes a single stone had to be held an entire day before the memory emerged from the stone. Indeed, there were countless stones in each basket, and if it were not for the greedy desire of each sister to beat the other in the basket making contest, they might have grown tired. Weeks went by and the sisters did not get up from the table except to stoke the fire. Each was busy with her own memory stones, but, at the same time, each took note of what the other was learning too. They didn't eat. They didn't sleep. Months went by and then years. Yet the sisters still had no notion of the time they had been sitting at the table, so concerned were they that one should not learn more basket making secrets from the memory stones than the other.

"I am getting tired," proclaimed the second Toad Sister at last.

"Me too," said the first Toad Sister. But this first Toad Sister saw that the second Toad Sister was bluffing. She saw that next the second Toad Sister would suggest that they close their eyes and rest awhile—at which time her sister was planning to steal her basket once and for all and then drag her to the door and lock her out of the house. Thus, the first Toad Sister thought, I will go along with her plan but I will open my eyes first and then steal her basket and throw her out. This time I will be the one to beat her at her own game. But, of course, the second sister knew what the other was thinking. What happened next was that each of the sisters jumped up and reached for the other's basket. They crashed into each other. The baskets fell from the table, which collapsed under the weight of the wrestling sisters, the memory stones spilling to the floor. The furious sisters fought one another with all their might. They rolled back and forth across the floor. At one point, they bumped into the fire. When at long last they had stopped fighting, their house had burned down. They found themselves standing where their kitchen had been, surrounded by the horrified villagers. Attached to each of the Toad Sisters' bodies were the countless memory stones.

The shocked villagers could not believe their eyes. Long ago Rain had disappeared from the village. The villagers thought Rain had run off with all of their memories, but they could not understand why. They figured that they had offended her in some way. They sang songs, tried to coax her back to the village from wherever she was hiding. Without her the people were lost. They forgot how to hunt. They forgot where to gather berries and acorns. They forgot how to care for the land. Without their memory stones they could do nothing. Bushes grew wild, uncared for, then withered away. Bulbs refused to sprout anew each spring. The Mountain was barren. What old baskets remained in the village—the baskets the villagers lined up before Rain's vacant house—sat empty, for there was no harvest. Now they knew what had happened. The twin Toad Sisters had stolen Rain's beautiful baskets containing the memory stones. No wonder Rain had disappeared. How could she continue to live amongst the villagers? How could she trust that someone else might not sneak into her house and make off with the beautiful baskets?

The Toad Sisters were equally amazed. The villagers were bone thin and hungry. The hills all around were naked. At the same time, the Toad Sisters were frightened, for they could see that the desperate villagers were about to rush them and pluck the memory stones from their skin. And just when complete madness was about to break out, Coyote, the headman, stepped forward with his wise nephew Chicken Hawk and commanded the people to control themselves and keep still.

"Step away from the ashes of your house," Coyote ordered the guilty twin Toad Sisters, whose bodies were speckled with the former memory stones.

As the twin sisters stepped out into the open, into the cool air, their skin tightened, causing the memory stones to fall from their bodies onto the ground. Again, the desperate villagers began to rush for the stones, but once more Coyote halted them.

"Listen," he said to the anxious crowd. "We no longer have Rain to keep our memories. Now each person must keep his or her own memory stone. Some of you will have to share memory stones. From this day forward, not only will we have to keep our own memories, but we'll also have to share our memories to put the Mountain back in order. If life does not return to the Mountain, if we are not successful, we shall certainly die."

Then Coyote told the people to line up in an orderly fashion to retrieve their stones. But as people picked up their stones, the stones disappeared just as quickly in their hands.

That was when Chicken Hawk, Coyote's wise nephew, stepped forward and spoke thus: "Do not worry. The memories are now inside your heads. That is where they will live from this day forward. And, that way, with the memories inside your heads, no one will be able to see them and be tempted again to steal."

"But what of Rain?" asked one of the villagers. "Will she ever return to us? She was the kindest of all people. We miss her terribly."

"I don't know," answered Chicken Hawk. "No doubt she has gone quite far away."

"Well then," said the villager. "What of these no-good twin Toad Sisters? What must we do with them? What punishment must they suffer?"

Chicken Hawk looked to Coyote, and the two of them began to confer. Wanting the twin sisters to be severely punished, the people anxiously waited for Coyote's decision regarding the Toad Sisters' fate.

It was Chicken Hawk who spoke first. "You two sisters have indeed done a terrible thing. You stole something that was not yours. But even after you stole those beautiful baskets, didn't you see the secret they contained? Didn't you see the important lesson when you first discovered Mouse's secret for her winning baskets? Mouse used leftover string. The secret to the perfect basket was to use whatever was left over. For several years we had leftover string. Before, there was leftover redbud bark for your beautiful designs. We are to share, each to our own abilities, each from our own memories. In time, you might have won the basket making contest again. But in the meantime you should have followed what your own memory showed you and worked harder. By cheating, by taking someone else's memory, you threw the entire Mountain out of order. You forgot other people. You even forgot yourselves and fought one another."

"So what is their punishment?" hollered the villager again.

"Well," said Coyote, starting to deliver the twin sister's sentence...But before he could continue, a voice came from the sky. The villagers looked up. They were so focused on Coyote and the twin Toad Sisters that they had not seen the thick rolling clouds that had gathered overhead.

"These twin Toads have suffered enough. I shall forgive them," the voice called, and it was none other than the lovely voice of Rain. Yes, see how their bodies are covered with spots and warts where the stones stuck to their skin. These girls will remain full of spots and warts forever. Take pity on them. Forgive them also as I have. Look at them and thank them for the important memory of this story."

The people, regardless of their animosity toward the twin Toad Sisters, obeyed Rain's command from the clouds and forgave the sisters.

"But will you ever come back to live with us?" the villagers cried to the clouds.

"Yes, but not exactly as before," answered Rain. "Don't worry. I still know all your memories. But I must live up here now. I will live in the clouds and ride on the wind. You need me now more than ever to help you bring the Mountain back to life, and I must do it from here. Each year during the winter, and at other times too, I shall return to help you replenish this beautiful Mountain."

"Oh, please come back," the villagers cried.

"Listen," said Rain, "ask the Toad Sisters to sing thus:

Mother, your twin daughters call

Spotted

A million memories

Please come

Mother, your twin daughters call

Spotted

A million memories

Please, please return

And that was what happened: The twin Toad Sisters began to sing. And, lo and behold, large wet drops fell from the clouds, and the people rejoiced.

The people obeyed their memories. The plants and trees grew again. And everyone knows to be forgiving and kind to those two spotted, ugly twin sisters, for only they can call Rain from the clouds.

Part 13

After Answer Woman finished telling the story about Rain, the twin sisters headed up the Mountain to their home amidst the branches of a bay laurel tree, for indeed not a moment after Answer Woman finished talking, huge raindrops fell from the clouds. Later that afternoon, when the downpour had subsided, the twin sisters returned to their spot atop the fence on Gravity Hill. Sun peeked through the parting clouds and the two sisters warmed themselves in its slender rays of light.

"I am thinking over the story you just told—about Rain keeping all of the memories," Question Woman said.

"That's good," answered Answer Woman. "The stories are here in the world for us to think about them."

"Well, at the end of the story all of the memories were given to the people, and everyone got to keep their memories inside their own heads."

"Yes, so what is your question?" asked Answer Woman.

"Why don't I have mine—why don't I have my memory?"

"Ah, but Sister, you do have your memory. You remember where our home is in the bay laurel tree. In fact, you just led us up the Mountain and then back to the fence here on Gravity Hill. You know where to gather acorns. You know where the most beautiful poppies grow every spring."

"But why can't I remember the stories? Why are you the one who gets to remember them?"

"Remember—I told you before—that the stories live in the air like seeds. Only your questions can bring them forth, like water on seeds in the ground. And then, when the stories come forth, I hear the words, what the story is saying, and I tell you what I hear. You water the seeds and then I tell you what flowers have come up. Do you understand?"

"Yes, but why can't I ask the questions and then get the stories myself? Why can't you ask the questions yourself and then get the stories?"

"You and I are here to remind the people of this beautiful Mountain that each one of us needs the other..."

"Oh, that again," complained Question Woman, interrupting her sister.

"Please listen...Each tree, each animal is important, just as each person in a family is important. We are all one family, after all. We can't forget one another and think we can go about this Mountain alone."

"Yes, I've heard that too, Sister," Question woman continued to complain.

"Well, this you haven't heard," said Answer Woman, "and here is the answer to your question: If either one of us had all the questions and all the answers, we might forget one another. We might forget the questions and the answers too. We are fixed this way so that we are reminded that we need one another...And every time the people hear us asking questions and telling stories, we are showing this important and essential truth—that even the stories cannot exist alone, neither the questions nor the stories. They go together, like everything else here on this Mountain."

"Yes, I think I understand now. Just as you were saying: I'm the one who must water the seeds that sprout the stories, and you are the one who tells what flowers come up—you tend the garden. We can't do the other person's job. We each have our job, our part to play. We are fixed that way, you and me."

"Yes, Sister, you understand. And the job we do together is very important. Don't forget that the people need the stories to live well, but, at the same time, the stories need the people—the stories need us if they are to come forth and have life too."

"All right, then how did we get this way? How did we get fixed the way we are?"

"Oh, Sister, you have just put your finger on our story, the story of you and me."

"Well?"

"Okay then, here we go...Listen."

Old Man Crow Asks His Twin Daughters to Gossip

*O*ne day in the village a handsome young couple announced that they would be married. Pronghorn, the young man, though rather small and slight of build, was not only a very hard worker but the fastest runner in the village. Indeed, he was a worthy suitor. Mourning Dove was the fair young maiden of his dreams. Kind and gentle, and notably beautiful in appearance, Mourning Dove was occasionally sad on account of the fact she had lost both of her parents when she was very young. Sometimes, in the middle of the morning or late afternoon, the villagers would hear her alone in the brush, crying for her lost parents. It was for that reason—because Mourning Dove was an orphan—that Coyote, the headman of the village, immediately stepped forward and offered to give her away.

"My lovely wife Frog Woman and I will host the wedding," Coyote said. "Furthermore, I would like some of you here in the village to make necklaces for the wedding. Mourning Dove can pick whichever necklace she feels will best match her wedding dress. Her bridesmaids can then pick over the other beautiful necklaces, finding whichever one they feel will go best with their dresses. We will make this a beautiful day for my adopted daughter and her fine fellow, Pronghorn."

Immediately several villagers came forth and volunteered to make necklaces. Coyote was pleased, and the happy engaged couple thanked the volunteers in advance for their generous efforts. Then the volunteers went off alone to gather what materials they needed; each of them already had an idea of the kind of necklace they would make.

It was nightfall by the time they returned to the village. They sat around a fire and showed one another what they had come back with to make their necklaces.

Holding up a handful of blue dick flowers, Rabbit said, "I will string together these beautiful flowers and make a necklace the color of the sky, and it will be lovely."

Then Gopher, holding up a handful of long sedge roots, said, "I will twine together these long roots and make a necklace the color of the earth, and it will be lovely."

Holding up a handful of empty spotted quail eggs, Raccoon said, "I will string together these beautiful shells and make a necklace the color of a rocky creek bed, and it will be lovely."

Then Fox held up a handful of robin's eggs, saying, "And with these beautiful blue shells I will make a necklace the color of lupine flowers on a hillside, and it will be lovely."

Then Elk, holding up a handful of deer bones, said, "And with these beautiful white deer bones I will make a necklace that people will be able to see for miles around, and it will be especially lovely."

At long last Squirrel spoke. Holding up a handful of twigs, Squirrel said, "I will string together these little twigs and make a necklace as black and shiny as obsidian, and it will be lovely."

"Why didn't you just use obsidian if you wanted a necklace to look like obsidian?" inquired Fox.

"I guess because I just didn't think of using obsidian," answered Squirrel.

"What kind of answer is that?" asked Raccoon, laughing with the others at Squirrel.

"The only answer I have," said Squirrel. "What do you want me to do, lie and make up a story?"

The others continued laughing, but Squirrel ignored them. He put his head down and, still ignoring the others, began stringing together his handful of twigs into a necklace.

Finally, Elk said, "We have laughed long enough. It is late, and we should go to bed. Besides, it is dark, and even with the fire it will be too difficult to see what we are doing. In the morning we will be able to see better—so that our necklaces don't turn out as silly as Squirrel's."

All together the villagers laughed again and then headed to their homes for the night, agreeing to meet again in the morning. Squirrel said to himself, "Yes, it is dark and I better go home too." He put away the work he had started and then went off, following the others.

Elk, however, did not go directly home. He stopped to see his friend Old Man Crow, which was not unusual since Elk often visited with Old Man Crow in the evenings to catch up on the day's news, and to gamble. Elk told Old Man Crow about the upcoming wedding of Pronghorn and Mourning Dove. They were seated at Old Man Crow's dinner table, with the light from a candle flickering on their faces. Old Man Crow always kept a candle burning, as he looked forward to Elk's visits and the two of them playing the stick game. Old Man Crow liked to play the stick game—he liked to gamble— but he wasn't a particularly lucky gambler.

"Oh, who would want to marry Mourning Dove?" Old Man Crow said. "She spends too much time in the woods crying for her dead parents."

"Pronghorn wants to marry her," Elk reminded Old Man Crow. "He told all of us today, 'I will make Mourning Dove happy. I will understand when she cries and I will give her the loving home she needs and deserves.'"

"That's what Pronghorn said?"

"That's what he said," answered Elk.

"Well, who else would have Mourning Dove but a skinny, weak fellow like Pronghorn?" said Old Man Crow.

Then Old Man Crow began to relate a story that his twin daughters had told him earlier that same evening. While gathering pine nuts further down the Mountain, the twin sisters had come upon several women from the village at the foot of the Mountain. The place was called Cotati Village. The people from the village near Copeland Creek on the top of the Mountain were interested in news of Cotati Village if for no other reason than that many suitable bachelors and beautiful maidens lived there. The twin Crow Daughters told their father of a fabulous tale the Cotati women had told them regarding a fair maiden who had two brothers competing for her hand. Apparently, this fair maiden, who was well known throughout the region, told the brothers that whichever one could run to the ocean and back the fastest would be the one to win her hand. The brothers set off; but, while they were gone, and were only halfway to the ocean, this maiden married the brothers' cousin, who, as it turned out, had all along been her secret love.

Elk listened to the story, but, as he listened, he plopped a small leather sack on the table.

"What's in the sack?" Old Man Crow asked, even before he was completely finished with his daughters' story.

Elk then emptied the sack and out poured a handful of beautiful quartz crystals. These crystals glistened in the candlelight.

"Let's start our stick game now," Elk said.

"You want to gamble those beautiful quartz crystals?" Old Man Crow asked, surprised. "But I have nothing that great to gamble in return."

"Oh, don't worry," Elk said. "You are not a very good gambler; and if you start to win too many of the crystals, we can stop playing."

Old Man Crow was dazzled by the quartz crystals, as he was always attracted by shiny objects. Yet he had never seen shiny objects as dazzling as these beautiful quartz crystals. Opposite the pile of quartz crystals Old Man Crow placed a pile of plain creek pebbles, which was what the two men normally played with when they gambled. Then he put the wooden staves for the stick game on the table, and the two men began to play. One game after the next Old Man Crow continued to win.

"Well, we better stop," Elk said. "Your luck must be particularly good this evening. Look, I only have one quartz crystal left, and soon it will be yours also."

Indeed, Elk only had one quartz crystal left, and right under Old Man Crow's eyes was the handful of crystals he had won, glistening in the candlelight.

"Well, let me see if I can win that last crystal," Old Man Crow said.

"As you wish," answered Elk.

And then, not surprisingly now, Old Man Crow won the last beautiful quartz crystal.

"Here, you must keep these," Old Man Crow said. "Take them back. They are beautiful and they are valuable. My luck tonight was too unusual."

"You keep them," said Elk, seeing Old Man Crow still gazing upon the beautiful stones.

"Buy why?"

"Well, I have a little favor to ask of you...I want to make sure that my necklace is the one Mourning Dove chooses to wear on her wedding day. Tomorrow, when we gather to make the necklaces, I want your twin daughters to sit near the circle where we will be working, and I want them to start telling stories. I want them to gossip. Have one of them tell the other the story they just told you about the maiden from Cotati Village—as that story is a particularly good one and will keep their attention. That way, the necklace makers will be distracted, and, at the end of the day, when Coyote calls forth Mourning Dove to pick one of the necklaces, mine will be the only one finished and she will have to pick mine."

Old Man Crow knew that Elk had always had a soft spot in his heart for Mourning Dove and that Elk was terribly hurt when Mourning Dove chose Elk's cousin Pronghorn over Elk. Why else had Old Man Crow suggested that Mourning Dove spent too much time crying and therefore would not make a good wife? Old Man Crow did not want Elk to think he had lost such a fine maiden. Any why else did Old Man Crow mention that Pronghorn was skinny and weak? He didn't want Elk to feel badly about himself after Mourning Dove chose Pronghorn instead of him. But now Old Man Crow could see that he had been tricked by Elk.

"That wasn't luck this evening. You tricked me. You let me keep winning," said Old Man Crow, "and now you are tempting me with these crystals in order to get me to go along with your plan to use my twin daughters...Furthermore, you have plans to use that necklace to put a love spell on Mourning Dove so that at the last moment she has a change of heart and marries you instead of Pronghorn."

"You are right about the first part," admitted Elk. "But you are wrong about the second part—I have no intention of putting a spell on Mourning Dove. I know that she truly loves Pronghorn and that if I put a spell on her, I still wouldn't be the one she truly loved. I only want her and the villagers to remember me on the wedding day. I want people far and near to see the deer bone necklace and know that I only wish her well."

"But you can do that yourself," said Old Man Crow.

Elk and Old Man Crow continued to talk back and forth for the longest time, far into the night. Old Man Crow told Elk that he was being prideful, even if all he wanted to do was have Mourning Dove and the villagers think that he no longer cared for Mourning Dove. Again, he told Elk to just let things be. But as he talked to Elk, Old Man Crow could not take his eyes off of the quartz crystals still glistening ever so brightly in the candlelight.

"All right then," Old Man Crow said, "I guess your giving Mourning Dove a necklace is not such a bad thing—even if you are doing so out of pride. But what guarantee do I have that you will not cast a spell on the unsuspecting Mourning Dove?"

"I will give you my black cap," said Elk. "Without this black cap, with nothing covering my head, people will know after a while that I must have done something wrong, that I didn't simply lose my cap. Should Mourning Dove fall in love with me after she takes my necklace, you may keep my cap as proof to everyone that indeed I had put a spell on the maiden, and then I would be severely punished by Coyote."

"All right then," Old Man Crow said, and he took the black cap from Elk.

The next morning the necklace makers gathered in a circle as planned. No sooner had they sat down than Old Man Crow's twin daughters appeared and seated themselves within earshot of the circle. Old Man Crow didn't tell the twin Crow Daughters why he wanted them to tell the gossipy story about the Cotati Village maiden, but simply asked that they sit close enough to the circle so that each and every necklace maker could hear them talking. "And make the story good—use a lot of juicy details so that you stretch the story out all day until Coyote comes to the circle," Old Man Crow instructed. And Old Man Crow gave each of his twin daughters two of the beautiful quartz crystals, which they greatly appreciated, for like their father they too were dazzled by shiny objects.

Moments after the obedient daughters left their father's house, Elk snuck up and showed himself at Old Man Crow's door.

"What do you want now?" Old Man Crow asked. "I've done what you wanted—I sent my twin daughters off to gossip."

"I want you to keep the deer bone necklace I have made. I worked on it all night and early this morning. I don't want the others to see that I have a finished necklace. I will sit listening to your twin daughters' story and appear distracted like everyone else. When Coyote arrives at the circle with Mourning Dove, I will quickly sneak off to retrieve the necklace."

Elk handed Old Man Crow a thatched box that contained the necklace, and Old Man Crow took the thatched box and then closed the door.

When Elk got to the circle of necklace makers, he found that they were so enraptured with the twin sisters' story that not a single one of them noticed he was late. The sisters had hardly begun the story, having just introduced the character of the Cotati maiden—again, a girl who was well known in the region—and the two handsome brothers who were competing for her hand. Already the twins were telling their tale with great flourish. One of the twins asked questions and the other twin answered, carrying the tale forward. The twin who asked questions did so often, repeating ear-catching details about what she had just been told. "Oh, dear Sister, why was the fair Cotati maiden wearing such a pretty red dress?"

By the time Coyote and Mourning Dove showed up near the end of the day, the twin Crow Sisters were just finishing their story.

"Oh, what has happened here?" Coyote asked, alarmed.

His adopted daughter Mourning Dove stood looking very sad, for she could see that not a single necklace had been made. Rabbit sat with her handful of blue dick flowers in her lap. Gopher sat with his long sedge roots, untouched. Raccoon's spotted quail eggshells were left on the ground next to his feet. It was the same with Fox's blue robin eggshells: They were just left on the ground, as if forgotten completely. Squirrel had his half-finished necklace made of small twigs in his lap, but he had added nothing to it, not a single twig, since leaving the circle the night before.

Coyote became more and more angry; certainly he suspected foul play. "Why have you been listening to these two gossipy girls?" he demanded to know.

No one could answer. They were ashamed that they had let meaningless gossip distract them from their task.

Then Coyote turned to the twin sisters, who had gotten up and were now making their way back to their father's house. He was about to address the sisters, but just then Elk showed up carrying two boxes, the thatched box in which he had placed his deer bone necklace, and a smaller box in which Old Man Crow said he had placed Elk's black cap.

"Wait! Wait!" Elk said, approaching the crowd. "I have a necklace for Mourning Dove to wear on her wedding day."

Everyone turned and looked with shock at Elk. Indeed, he had snuck away from the circle when he saw Coyote and Mourning Dove arriving. But, unbeknownst to him, by the time he arrived at Old Man Crow's house to retrieve the deer bone necklace, Old Man Crow had had a change of heart. He knew that plotting with Elk in order to trick the others was wrong. Furthermore, he knew that Coyote would suspect something wrong and consult with his wise nephew Chicken Hawk. "No doubt I will get caught," Old Man Crow said to himself. "After all, the ones gossiping near the circle of necklace makers were none other than my twin daughters. I must do what I can to make things right so that Elk cannot carry out his plan." And that was why Old Man Crow played a trick on Elk just then.

"I put your cap in the smaller box," Old Man Crow said, handing Elk a small, plain-looking box.

Elk took both the plain box and the thatched box. He was so excited that he didn't think to ask why Old Man Crow had given back his cap when he had agreed to let him keep it until Crow was certain that he hadn't used the necklace to put a spell on Mourning Dove. He was so excited he didn't notice that when he opened the smaller box what he took out and he placed on his head was the deer bone necklace, and what he was offering Mourning Dove, after opening the thatched box, was his cap. What Coyote and Mourning Dove and the astounded other necklace makers saw was a man with a crown of deer bones on his head, offering his cap as a necklace.

Everyone began to laugh wildly at the sight. Even the twin Crow Sisters had stopped and were laughing. But in no time a hush returned to the crowd, for everyone knew that something had gone terribly wrong. They looked back to a very irritated Coyote, who was joined now by his wise nephew Chicken Hawk.

"You necklace makers were tricked into listening to gossip," Coyote said. "Someone made a plan to have those loud-mouthed twin girls sit alongside you. No doubt, it was you," Coyote said, looking at Elk with his crown of deer bones and his cap in his hand.

"And me," admitted Old Man Crow, suddenly appearing in the middle of the crowd.

Old Man Crow told exactly what had happened, how he had been complicit in Elk's scheme. "I was tempted by the beautiful quartz crystals in this bag," Old Man Crow admitted, holding up the sack that contained the crystals.

Coyote conferred with his nephew Chicken Hawk and then turned back to the crowd.

"A bad deed has occurred," Coyote announced. "All of you have played a part in this bad deed, even if it was simply not paying attention to the necklaces you promised Mourning Dove and instead listening to gossip."

"I promise my daughters won't gossip again," offered a humiliated Old Man Crow.

"Your twin daughters will tell stories from now on," Coyote said to Old Man Crow. "Things have been fixed anew on this Mountain because of what has happened today...Your twin Crow Daughters will indeed keep talking, and they will keep talking just as they did here today, with one asking questions and one giving answers. The one asking questions will not remember answers, and the one giving answers will not be able to give answers without the questions. They will thus be known as Question Woman and Answer Woman. And what they will tell us—what one will ask about and one will answer— are the stories we need to remember. That way, if we are distracted by them again, we will only hear good stories. We will be reminded of what happened today and then hear the stories we need to know in order to live well on this Mountain."

Old Man Crow listened silently, accepting the fate of his twin daughters, one of whom already could not remember any answers, and the other of whom could not give any answers without a question.

"Here, take this bag of quartz crystals from me," Old Man Crow said to Coyote.

"No," Coyote said. "You at least have come forth and been honest. You keep those crystals and look at them any time you are tempted to do the wrong thing to gain a shiny object." Coyote looked to Old Man Crow's twin daughters. "Your father gave you each two of the crystals. You did not know that you had been part of Elk's plot, but you should not have been distracting others with idle gossip. I have put those shiny crystals in your eyes, and from now on you will have bright, shiny eyes no less beautiful than the glittering objects that attract you."

Then Coyote turned to Elk. "As for you, foolish one, you will keep that deer bone necklace right where it is—on your head. Prideful people think they deserve crowns like princes and kings. Why did you think you were so special that my adopted daughter should have chosen you to be her husband and that you didn't have to accept her choice?"

"I wasn't going to put a love spell on her, honest," pleaded Elk.

"I know that," said Coyote. My nephew and I have determined as much. But you wanted everyone to think you were still a big man, that you were special, by getting over your pride and making a beautiful necklace for Mourning Dove. The fact of the matter was that you were still prideful. You will look quite handsome with your crown of deer bones, but of course you will always be reminded of how you got them."

"I'm sorry," said Elk to Mourning Dove. Elk had dropped his cap with all of his trembling, and now he bent down to pick it up.

"Here, give that cap to me," said Coyote. "You won't need it anymore." Then Coyote gave the cap to Deer, who had walked up, hearing all of the commotion. "Deer, from now on you will wear Elk's cap and look quite handsome."

Everything seemed to be in its place now, but of course Mourning Dove did not have a single necklace, save the half-finished band of twigs she had taken from Squirrel. "I will take this one," said Mourning Dove. "It will be fine."

"Do not worry, Daughter. My nephew and I have conferred about the necklaces too. You will have the necklace of your choice and so will your bridesmaids." And, having said as much, Coyote commanded the necklace makers to pick up the materials—the blue dick flowers, the long sedge roots, the quail eggshells, the robin eggshells—that they had left on the ground, and to begin bright and early the next day making necklaces.

A week later Mourning Dove and Pronghorn had a joyous wedding. The entire village was there. Pronghorn turned out to be a good husband indeed, providing the lovely Mourning Dove the safe home that she needed and deserved, and he was always understanding of her when she felt lonely for her lost parents. Oh, and if you see the little black band on Mourning Dove's neck, you will know which necklace she wore in her wedding. That fateful day before her wedding, she kept Squirrel's half-finished necklace of twigs the color of obsidian, and, in the end, found it the most beautiful.

Part 14

ſome months later when it was spring and warm sun lit the green hills, the twin sisters, Question Woman and Answer Woman, found themselves again at their favorite spot atop the wooden fence on Gravity Hill. They stretched and yawned, basking in the sun's warmth. Spears of new lupine and golden poppy buds bobbed in a gentle breeze. A flock of chirping bluebirds landed on the fence alongside the sisters, then flew off again, their fluttering wings the same blue as the sky.

"We made it through another winter. We told a lot of stories, didn't we?" said Question Woman.

"Yes," answered Answer Woman, "but the stories are endless. There are an infinite number of them, for remember that everything you see on this glorious Mountain is at the same time a story."

"You know what I don't like sometimes about the stories?" said Question Woman.

"What?"

"It seems that people are always getting punished for something."

"Well, people in the stories get punished if they do something greedy or selfish, yes. But there is so much more that the stories show us besides the punishment—and sometimes because of the punishment."

"Like what?"

"The stories teach us lessons..."

"Yes, I know that."

"Sister, you haven't let me finish...More than showing us a punishment for greedy or selfish behavior, the stories teach us that we can learn and change. If we make a mistake—and even if something bad happens to us—we can learn and change. We can change how we do things, and that is the way of all life."

"Can you give an example? You know I forget the stories."

"Think about how we got fixed the way we are, with one of us always forgetting the stories and the other one only telling the stories when the forgetting one asks. Our father, Old Man Crow, made a poor decision to go along with Elk's prideful scheme to impress Mourning Dove. In the end everyone in the story got punished. You and I got punished, true. We now live differently. We live better because of the punishment, because of how we changed then. You and I don't gossip anymore. The villagers didn't need gossip anymore; the villagers needed us to tell good stories and now we do. As I said, all of life is the same way. If water from a late spring rain washes a quail's nest away, the quail will pick a drier place next time to build her nest. As a tree grows, spreading its branches, the golden poppies underneath will keep moving to get out from underneath the shade in order to keep themselves full in the sun."

"Wow! That's important—learning to live with change."

"We have no choice, dear Sister. Things that don't learn and change die."

"Oh, that's a big question: Why must things die?"

"Well, in truth we don't really die—not in the stories. And, as the wise people on this Mountain tell us, the stories are more real than anything else. And it's the stories that make life everlasting, eternal. That large old oak tree that you see in the distance is a story as much or even more than it is a tree, more than just a big thing with a gnarled trunk and hanging branches. Even after the tree dies and another tree or something else grows up, the story remembers and tells what happened, tells about the changes. And remember, if we forget the story, say if we see the old oak tree as just a big thing with a gnarled trunk and hanging branches, if we forget that the tree is a living spirit with a story, we might lose a lesson important to our survival here."

"Yes, I understand."

"So as I was saying earlier, everything we see on this glorious Mountain is at the same time a living, talking story. In fact, when we look around we will see in all things something or someone who has lived before and continues to live."

"Like someone who has died?"

"Take, for example, the story of Coyote's two sons."

"Yes?"

"Well, those two sons died, or at least Coyote thought they did, and instead of dying they became something else."

"What happened?"

"Coyote did a selfish thing."

"I thought Coyote was a good leader."

"He was a good leader. But as a man he had a lot to learn so that he could be a good leader."

"What happened? What happened to his sons?"

"I knew you would ask. Listen."

Coyote Throws His Sons into the Sky

*L*ong, long ago, before Coyote was the headman of the village, he went looking for a wife. "If I am going to be headman, I surely need a good wife who will be my partner and friend," he told himself. Coyote was a handsome and ambitious young man. Already the villagers had their eye on him, thinking that one day in the near future they would elect him as their leader. "How will we know when Coyote is ready to take office?" Skunk asked the Council of Wise Women Governors, who determines such things. "We will know," answered the four Wise Women, "for he will do something that will show us that he is ready to assume his position as headman of our village. He will do something great."

Regarding finding a good wife, Coyote was doing everything right. He consulted four old men who gave young bachelors advice on what qualities a man must possess and utilize in order to be a good husband.

"Be kind," Yellow Jacket told him.

"Be warm, stay close to your wife," Flea told him.

"Be talkative, let her know when you are home," Blue Jay told him.

"Be hardworking," Bear told him.

And a fifth person, a woman named Hummingbird, told Coyote that he must follow his heart. "And one more thing,"

Hummingbird said. "Each good woman has a song and you must learn to hear that song and answer it with a special song that she will teach you, for only that way will you be her true husband."

"Thank you all for the good advice," Coyote told the four old men and Hummingbird.

Then Hummingbird said, "Make sure you listen well to your beloved's song," and the four old men agreed and reiterated Hummingbird's advice.

At long last Coyote found the young maiden he wished to marry; and, as you may already know, that fair maiden was none other than Frog Woman. Truth be known, Coyote had had his eye on Frog Woman all along and hoped that one day she would become his beloved wife. One afternoon, while Coyote was traveling through the hills, he came upon Frog Woman alone next to a pond of water and she was singing thus:

> *Clearing the reeds*
>
> *Pushing aside the swamp grass*
>
> *Dreaming*
>
> *Dreaming*
>
> *I am clearing the reeds*
>
> *Pushing aside the swamp grass*

Near the water

Near the water

Seeing a family

Coyote thought Frog Woman's song was the most beautiful song he had heard. His heart was so touched that for the longest time he was speechless.

"I've never known you sounded so lovely," he said at last.

"Oh, I didn't know you were there, listening behind the bushes," said Frog Woman, a bit startled. "I had my back to you."

"I didn't mean to startle you," said Coyote. "I was coming to see you anyway, and now my heart is touched..."

Frog Woman blushed.

Then Coyote said, "But I must tell you—and perhaps you already know—it is you who have touched my heart all along. No fair maiden on this Mountain has such beautiful big shiny eyes. Your eyes are so black and shiny I can see the green hills and blue Sky in them."

"Oh, you flatter me," said Frog Woman. "But you must know that beauty is not everything. What is most important is what lies in a person's heart."

"Oh, yes, and right now my heart is beating really fast," said Coyote. "So I must finally ask if you would so honor me and teach me a special song in order that I might answer the lovely song I heard you singing and become your true and good husband."

"The wise old men and Hummingbird have given you good advice," answered Frog Woman, and she began singing thus:

Near the water

Near the water

Your beloved friend

Seeing you

A partner I will be

Helping

Helping

Even with a million children helping still

And that way, singing, Coyote led Frog Woman back to the village and married her there. He built her a fine house of pine logs near the creek so at night she could be comforted by the sound of gurgling water and be reminded of her old home next to the pond in the hills. They lived there for a long time, and Frog Woman was much loved in the village. She was helpful to people and kind to everyone. Often her cousins, the two Toad Sisters, were sad, worried that they were too spotted and ugly for anyone to love. On several occasions Frog Woman sat outside her house, alongside the creek, talking to them all night long, assuring them that they were beautiful. "Your spots are marks of beauty," she told them, "and inside your hearts are beautiful songs and stories." By morning the Toad Sisters were always happy and confident again.

Though he didn't say anything to Frog Woman, Coyote was often bothered when she stayed out all night talking to her cousins. He preferred it when she was in the house with him. He thought the two Toad Sisters were ugly, and he consoled himself with the fact that Frog Woman didn't look like her cousins.

Meanwhile, the villagers wondered when the Council of Wise Women Governors would appoint Coyote as their headman. "When will Coyote be our chief?" the villagers asked.

For some time Coyote had been demonstrating good qualities for leadership. He settled arguments when people squabbled. He was a brave hunter and could lead other hunters far to the other side of the Mountain to gather food the villagers needed. He was an expert shot with a bow and arrow, and he was smart and as clever as could be.

Then Coyote and Frog Woman had two sons, handsome boys who were fat and healthy, for Frog Woman did a fine job caring for them, proving that indeed she was an excellent mother. But Coyote was beginning to feel left out. At night Frog Woman still often visited with her cousins, and much of the day she was preoccupied with the two boys, the younger one and the older one. She spent long hours making them clothes and warm blankets; each and every morning she made fresh, steaming acorn mush.

"What about me?" Coyote complained one evening after

Frog Woman put the boys to bed and was leaving to visit the Toad Sisters.

"Oh, now don't you worry," said Frog Woman. "A good wife takes care of her children and doesn't forget her cousins. And a good wife doesn't forget her husband. It's quite a job I have, isn't it? Have I forgotten you, dear Husband? Don't I still cook excellent meals? Don't we sit together still and share our thoughts and dreams? You know the answer, dear Husband."

Coyote did know the answer: Frog Woman was an excellent wife. In fact, in caring for the two sons and still consoling her insecure cousins, the Toad Sisters, Frog Woman proved more than ever what a fine person she was—truly suitable to be a chief's wife, for to all of the villagers she set a fine example of caring and kindness.

"Listen, Coyote," she said to him. "Come down to the creek in the mornings and help me prepare the boys' acorn mush. You don't have to spend so much time drinking tea. Come with me at night to visit my cousins; you could assure them of their worth and beauty too. You don't need to spend so much time at night sharpening your arrowheads. You have plenty of sharp arrowheads."

But Coyote didn't listen. One day while Frog Woman was out gathering pine nuts, Coyote took the two boys and with great force hurled them into the Sky. He threw each of them so hard that they disappeared behind the Sky's blue cover, completely out of sight. When Frog Woman arrived home, she asked where the boys were.

"They must have run off someplace," Coyote told her.

"Oh, they wouldn't go far," said Frog Woman.

After four days the boys still had not returned, and Frog Woman was beside herself with worry.

"Where are the boys?" she asked frantically.

"I took them and threw them into the Sky," Coyote said, "because you spend too much time with them."

Frog Woman cried and cried.

"Now you can spend more time with me," Coyote said.

But that was not what happened. On the fifth day Frog Woman packed her clothes and returned to her pond in the hills. Coyote followed her and begged her to come back, but she would not listen to him.

Coyote found he had even more trouble back at the village. People saw how upset their dear friend Frog Woman was, and now they too knew what Coyote had done with the two boys. "How can this man be our leader?" they asked. "He has not done something great but instead something terrible."

Coyote himself knew he had done something terrible. He knew he had made a great mistake. He went to his nephew Chicken Hawk for help. Chicken Hawk was very young then, but already he flew high in the Sky. Because he flew so high in the Sky, Chicken Hawk was a good friend of Thermal Wind, the great and wise old man whose invisible flowing beard carries all soaring birds high above the earth.

"Please," Coyote begged his nephew, "would you ask Thermal Wind to help me get my sons back? I have thrown them into the Sky, past its blue cover. I have done a terrible thing. But since Thermal Wind lives so close to Old Father Sky, maybe he could ask Old Father Sky what happened to my sons. Maybe Old Father Sky could find them and send them back to earth. That way I could get my wife Frog Woman back and once again have the Council of Wise Women Governors consider me as the villagers' leader."

"Well indeed what you have done doesn't sound good at all," said Chicken Hawk, "but I will go and consult with my old and wise friend Thermal Wind."

Chicken Hawk went off then. He was gone for several days. But when he returned he didn't have Coyote's two sons with him. Instead a very old man in white robes the color of his long hair was with Chicken Hawk.

"This is Thermal Wind," said Chicken Hawk. "We have some bad news."

The villagers gathered around—everyone except for Frog Woman, who remained at her pond in the hills. Coyote was beside himself with dread at the prospect of hearing bad news regarding his thrown-away sons.

"Please step forward," old man Thermal Wind said to Coyote.

Coyote, trembling with fear and trepidation, did as the old man bid him and stood in front of the large crowd of silent villagers.

"Oh, please," said Coyote, alone in front of the crowd, "don't tell me you haven't found my sons."

"Your sons are dead," said Thermal Wind.

Coyote was puzzled then. He had not heard of Death—nor had any of the villagers, and they were equally puzzled.

"Where is that?" asked Coyote, thinking that Death was a place he hadn't heard of.

"Listen carefully," said Thermal Wind. "Your sons will not return, at least not as you have known them. Because of what you have done, Death is now upon the Mountain. From now on, all things must die. People will grow old and die. Sometimes accidents will happen and people will die. Sometimes people will get lost and die. They won't ever come back, not exactly as they were before. When you threw your boys into the Sky, they became lost and died."

"Do you mean I killed my sons?" Coyote asked, shocked.

"You didn't know about Death. You didn't intend to kill your sons, because you didn't know yet that Death could happen, but still you must suffer the consequences."

"You mean I'll never see my sons again?"

"You will see your sons," answered Thermal Wind, "but, like I said, you won't see them the way you once did. There will be ways to remember and still see people after they are gone. There will be stories. People will sometimes change into things after they leave us, and we'll see those things. Some people will turn into rocks, others may turn into flowers or trees. But always it will be stories that remind us of them, of their lives and of what happened to them. Your boys will always remind us of how Death came to Sonoma Mountain.

But they will remind us of so much more when we see them. There will be so much light, and we will be able to see and appreciate life all the more."

"But where are they?"

Thermal Wind then pointed to the Sky. Coyote and the others looked up, and, with utter amazement, found in the Sky a huge golden ball of light.

"You see," said Thermal Wind, "I talked to Old Father Sky just as Chicken Hawk asked, and Old Father Sky went looking for your sons and found them behind a large rock. They were glowing there; they had died and turned into round glowing lights. He carried them back as far as he could, to his blue curtain. Thus, your oldest boy became the Sun, and your youngest the Moon. Sun will give us warmth and light. When Sun leaves at the end of each day, the younger boy, Moon, will then appear. Moon will shrink and expand again and again, leaving us at times with little light, but that is only to remind us that we must never forget him and his older brother, lest we be without light."

"But why couldn't Old Father Sky bring my sons all the way back to the village?"

"Because Old Father Sky doesn't ever come close to earth."

"What of my nephew?" pleaded Coyote. "Couldn't he carry them back?"

"They are too big now for Chicken Hawk to carry," answered Thermal Wind. "So they must stay where they are."

At that point, Coyote—understanding that he would never

see his two sons playing happily outside the pine-log house again or joyously singing alongside their mother as she worked and visited amongst the villagers—began to cry.

"Now you know the sorrow of Death," said Thermal Wind.

"My heart is broken," said Coyote. "And what of my lovely wife? I suppose after what I have done she will never come back."

"That will be for you to find out," said Thermal Wind. "But maybe now you can see that you were not such a good husband. You were not always warm and kind. You were selfish, often thinking only of what you wanted. You didn't listen to Hummingbird's advice to listen carefully to your beloved's special song. Didn't you hear the word 'helping'? Didn't you sing that you would be a partner, helping? Nor did you listen to your beloved Frog Woman when she told you that beauty is not everything, that it must not be the only thing that appeals to your heart."

"Oh, oh," cried Coyote. "How horrible I have been! My beloved Frog Woman told me that what is most important is what lies in a person's heart. I kept looking at her pretty big eyes, listening to my own heart racing, instead of seeing how truly beautiful she was. I didn't see that in Frog Woman's heart lies all the caring and kindness in the world. Oh dear, think how that caring heart must hurt now that she's lost her sons."

Coyote himself hurt so badly that he collapsed in a pool of tears. And that way, with Coyote crying uncontrollably,

Thermal Wind took leave of the village, and Chicken Hawk flew up and followed after him.

Then, just before the villagers began to leave, the Council of Wise Women Governors stepped forward and made a pronouncement that shocked everyone, for in unison the four Wise Women said, "Coyote is now ready to be our leader."

"What do you mean?" protested Skunk, speaking up before the others. "What great deed has Coyote done? What has he done other than throw away his two sons?"

"He has learned to see and understand the heart of another person," the Wise Women, speaking again in unison, answered. "That is the greatest accomplishment for anyone, for a husband, and for a leader. Coyote has seen his wife's heart and felt his own heart—now he can know the hearts of all the people he will lead."

Coyote, now kneeling on the ground, could not believe his ears. Yet he knew what the four Wise Women Governors said was true. Feeling his hurting heart, he rose to his feet. Later, at a formal ceremony, Coyote humbly accepted his position as chief of the village. But not before he went looking for Frog Woman.

He found her again at her pond in the hills and sang to her thus:

> *Near the water*
>
> *Near the water*
>
> *Your beloved friend*

Seeing you

A partner I will be

Helping

Helping

Even with a million children helping still

Frog Woman turned and saw him. She knew his heart had changed, and she knew this time he was true. But, as it turned out, she continued to spend much of her time at the pond, but it didn't matter, because Coyote would always be there with her. And, oh, did the words to the song ever turn out true, for Frog Woman and Coyote had many more children—frog children. Every year, after the first heavy rain, you can hear them singing, millions of them, all over the Mountain. And Coyote still thinks of his first two sons; sometimes at night he howls for them. But he knows where he can always see them. As Frog Woman sits the way she does, always looking up at the Sky, all Coyote has to do is find the boys, one during the day and the other at night, reflected in her lovely big eyes.

Part 15

One day around noontime the twin Crow Sisters, Question Woman and Answer Woman, stopped to rest at their favorite spot atop the fence on Gravity Hill. All morning they had been flying about Sonoma Mountain enjoying the warm spring sun. They saw the hills awash in color, broad patches of gold and purple flowers like radiant carpets amidst the green grass. They heard birds singing loudly in the trees. Even now, perched on the fence rail, they could hear the birds singing and see animals going about their business. Deer grazed on a nearby hill while their fawns slept peacefully in the tall grass. A mother wild turkey crossed the road followed by a line of fuzzy turkey chicks. A buzzard soared overhead crossing paths with a Cooper's hawk; and, down the road, a husky bobcat sharpened his claws on a fence post. At this moment, the world seemed brighter and busier than ever before, even than on other spring days.

"I don't remember the Mountain so bright with color and so busy with all of these birds and animals going about. All of the animals in the stories seem to be here now, and all of the flowers and trees," remarked Question Woman.

"You often don't remember things," answered her sister, Answer Woman. "That is why you have so many questions—and I don't have answers without your questions, lest you forget that too. It is the very middle of spring today. A day like this day makes us think of all the stories because we see all of the birds and animals in the stories."

Question Woman thought a moment, then gazed out upon the bright Mountain again. On a distant hillside Question Woman saw a herd of white-faced cows with their white-faced calves. Clouds of starlings swooped and fell in the sky above the cows and calves.

"Wait!" said Question Woman. "I don't remember any stories about cows or starlings."

"Or about wild turkeys," added Answer Woman.

"Where did they come from?"

"They are new animals," answered Answer Woman. "People brought them here, but, don't worry, they have stories too. Everything has a story. Every blade of grass, every flower."

"But where did the people get the new animals? Where did the people find them?"

"The new animals came back with the people who left this wondrous Mountain long ago...But we are getting ahead of ourselves, Sister. The question you should be asking is how did animals take their present forms as we see them today, and how did people as we see them now come about in the first place? How did Deer grow four slender long legs and Bear four sharp claws? How did people get hands and feet and a thatch of hair on top of their heads and go about as they do?"

"There's a story for that too?"

"Oh, yes, an important story. Look there," said Answer Woman, nodding with her shiny beak to a man coming up the road on a bicycle. "He didn't just come up here from the bottom of the Mountain. He has a story, like all human beings, that goes back to that ancient time when all of the animals were still people. Coyote changed things around. Birds grew wings, animals got hooves and claws..."

"Well, what happened?" asked a perplexed Question Woman.

"That's the important story. Listen."

Coyote Creates

People

Coyote's wife, Frog Woman, often spent the night with their children at the pond where Frog Woman lived before she married Coyote. This was particularly true in spring, when the many frog children were busy and needed Frog Woman's full attention. Ever since Coyote made the dreadful mistake of throwing the couple's first two children into the sky, one child becoming the Moon and the other the Sun, he knew to respect her and the time she spent with their children. Nonetheless, in the evenings when Frog Woman was not with him, he found himself anxious and lonesome. What am I going to do with myself? he thought.

He told his wise nephew Chicken Hawk of his problem.

"I need friends," Coyote complained. "I sit home at night with nothing to do, no one to talk to."

"Ah, but Uncle, you are chief of the village now. You are admired by everyone. All of the people of this village are your friends. Have you thought of going to visit with any of them while Frog Woman is away with the children?'

"Yes," answered Coyote. "I have already thought of your suggestion and gone to visit some of the villagers, my good friends, but they are always busy and seem to have something else to do. My good friend Old Man Crow gambles all night with Elk, and what can I do but sit by the lamp and watch?

The seven Bat Brothers, my hunting partners, all they do is sit outside looking up at their wives, the seven stars of the Big Dipper, and what can I do but sit out in the cold with them?"

"Well, there's something to be learned by the things your friends do—you can remember and think about their stories as you sit with them at night. Night is a good time to think about stories, after all. And, certainly, it comforts your friends to know you are there."

"Oh, Nephew, I know all of their stories, so what?" Coyote continued to grumble.

Chicken Hawk saw that he was getting nowhere with his uncle, so he had to think of something else.

"If visiting people proves unsatisfying to you, Uncle, why don't you make something beautiful for your lovely wife or for someone else? You are an expert maker of headdresses and belts. When you go to visit your friends at night, take the feathers and beads you need to make a headdress or belt with you. While Old Man Crow and Elk gamble you can work on your lovely gift; in between their stick games, they will see your beautiful work and marvel. The seven Bat Brothers cannot stare up at their wives all night; when they look down from the sky, they will see your beautiful work and marvel likewise. You will stay busy while your friends are busy; and then afterwards, all of you will have something to talk about— all the while keeping each other company. You won't be alone; you'll be together in the same room."

"Sounds all right," said Coyote, thinking about his nephew's suggestion. "You don't think I'll bother them?"

"Oh, goodness no, Uncle. Just tell them what you're doing. People like to be together. Isn't that what's bothering you? You don't want to be alone?"

"Yes, true. You're right. I don't want to be alone," answered Coyote.

"Just remember that you once wanted too much attention from your wife and got yourself into trouble. And, before that, you got yourself into trouble when you wanted too much attention from the villagers. Remember the time you made a headdress so big that it crushed you?"

"Yes, I remember. But now I am just lonely. I just want someone to talk to when my wife is gone. What is wrong with that?"

"Nothing, as long as you don't think only of yourself. You are our chief: You of all people must always keep the villagers in mind with whatever you do. Now why don't you try what I have suggested? Get busy making a lovely headdress or belt."

Coyote knew to listen to his nephew. That evening Coyote went to the home of Old Man Crow. Coyote had gathered a sack strips of leather, a handful of clamshell disc beads, and a handful of abalone pendants for a belt. He figured a belt would be easier and faster to make than a headdress; and, that way, he would have something for his friends to talk about that much sooner. Just as Chicken Hawk had predicted, Old Man Crow and his gambling partner Elk were happy to have Coyote work alongside them while they played their stick games, and, in between games, Old Man Crow and Elk marveled at the belt Coyote had started to make. The clamshell disc beads looked like stars on the leather sash, and the abalone pendants glinted like tiny rainbows.

"Oh, how beautiful," said Old Man Crow.

"You are the best belt maker of all," said Elk.

The next night Coyote visited the seven Bat Brothers. They too were happy to have Coyote working alongside them. They stared up at their wives, the seven stars of the Big Dipper, for the longest time, but at long last they looked down and saw what a marvelous belt Coyote was making. Even more of the belt was finished by this time.

"Oh, how beautiful," said the Bat Brothers in unison. "Coyote, you are the best belt maker of all."

That way, night after night, Coyote visited his many friends, until the belt was finished. Then he went back to visit Old Man Crow and Elk, where he had started.

"Oh, you have finished the belt," said Old Man Crow after he ended a game of sticks with Elk. "It is absolutely beautiful."

"Yes," said Elk. "It is so beautiful. Who are you going to give it to?"

The next night Coyote went to see the seven Bat Brothers. After looking up at their seven wives in the sky for the longest time, they too saw that Coyote had finished the belt.

"Oh, the belt is absolutely beautiful," they said in unison, seeing the long sash adorned with disc beads like stars and dangling pendants like tiny rainbows. "Who are you going to give it to?"

Night after night, as he visited one friend and then another, each of them said the same thing, "Oh, how beautiful the belt is," and, just like Old Man Crow and the seven Bat Brothers, they asked, "Who are you going to give the belt to?"

Coyote had not thought about who was going to get the beautiful belt. Had he decided to give the belt to his wife, Frog Woman, or was that Chicken Hawk's idea? When he finished the belt, he had assumed that all of his friends would stop what they were doing and have a long conversation with him about the belt, maybe asking him about how he came up with the intricate design of shell discs and pendants that made the belt so beautiful. Or at least they might just continue to marvel at its beauty a little while longer. Well, thought Coyote, I am going to go back and hold the belt for them to look at again and see if they have anything more to say.

And that's what he did—went back with the finished belt to each of his friends.

"Oh, the belt is absolutely lovely," Old Man Crow said after he finished a game of sticks with Elk. "I would feel so proud wearing a belt like that." Elk then said the same thing, and so did the seven Bat Brothers: "I would feel so proud wearing a belt like that." And, night after night, visiting each of his many friends, he heard again and again the same thing: "Oh, what an absolutely beautiful belt. I would feel so proud wearing a belt like that."

Now I suppose I will have to make each of them a belt,

Coyote thought to himself. Isn't that what they want? Well, if that is what I must do to get them to talk with me more, then I will make each of them a belt, Coyote decided. But after he gathered numerous handfuls of clamshell disc beads and abalone pendants, he began to think again. Sitting alone in his house with leather strips and clamshell disc beads and abalone pendants in a pile on the table before him, he pictured himself night after night sitting alongside Old Man Crow while making a belt. The same for Elk and for the seven Bat Brothers. It would be years before he finished a beautiful belt for each of his many friends. And for what, he wondered, only to have them look away from whatever they were doing and mention for only a moment how lovely the belt looked and then thank him for it after he gave it to them? "Nothing will be different," he said to himself. "If I add up all the time I will be sitting alongside each of my friends without talking it will be years—years of silence." He thought again and again of each of his friends. Then he got an idea.

That next evening Coyote went to see Old Man Crow and Elk.

"Old Man Crow," Coyote addressed the old man with the gambling staves. "Give me a special stone—some small object that most represents you. With that special object I can fashion a belt that will most suit you...It may take me a while, but you will have a special belt with your object as its centerpiece."

"Oh, that sounds wonderful," Old Man Crow said. "I would be so honored if you made me such a belt." He then found a chunk of obsidian and gave it to Coyote. "Here, my friend," said Old Man Crow. "This chunk of black stone looks most like me."

Next Elk got up from the table and returned with a small square of oak bark. "Here, Coyote," Elk said, placing the oak bark in Coyote's hand. "This piece of bark looks most like me."

Coyote did not stick around then. He went to the house of each of his friends and asked that they likewise give him a special object in order that he might fashion a belt that would best suit them. In the morning, when he returned exhausted to his home, he found his leather sack with the cache of special objects was so heavy he could not lift it to his table, so he left the sack just inside his door. He rested awhile, and then when it was dark again he went to visit Bobcat.

"Bobcat," Coyote said, "you are the keeper of the shape-shifting songs. I have so many belts to make I need one of your songs to help me. If I have one of your shape-shifting songs, I can finish the belts in one night and that way give each of my friends their special belts right away—they won't have to wait weeks or months, even years."

Bobcat knew of Coyote's plan to make special belts—Bobcat had himself handed Coyote a ball of tawny clay the night before.

"Well," said Bobcat, "these shape-shifting songs are powerful. Remember, when you sing them, you can change from one form to another. Therefore the songs must be sung with great thought and care. You know how they work: You sing the song over yourself—or a special object, in your case. Then you say out loud what you want the object to become. You must always return yourself—or, in your case, the special object—home. Then it can return to its original form."

Then Coyote said, "You see, my plan is to give each person his or her special belt—so I don't care about the special objects turning back into themselves. I will just sing the song and say out loud: 'Special belt with special object as its centerpiece.' Will that work?"

Bobcat thought a moment. Before he could answer Coyote, Coyote said, "You see, I am very lonely at night when my wife is gone. I want to visit with my friends. The belts will give us something to talk about. I won't have to sit in silence beading and feathering the belts forever if you will give me a shape-shifting song."

"Well, you are taking a shortcut," said Bobcat. "But that is what a shape-shifting song can do—help us to do extraordinary things when necessary. I don't see any harm now with your plan. Yes, the song will work for you. But I would suggest that first you spend one night just singing the song and thinking about what you want to do. Think about whom you are doing this for and your reasons for doing it. Remember the lessons you've learned in the past and the mistakes you have made, Coyote. And you must know that what someone turns into always remains a part of him. The same is true for any objects you wish to change from one thing to another. Something about them will behave like you. The nature of the person singing the songs lives on in a changed person or object. The physical form of something may change but not its character. On the second night, after you have practiced singing and have thought about these things, then sing again and say out loud what you want."

Coyote nodded in agreement and then said, "I know these songs are very expensive. I will trade my beautiful belt that you and all my friends have so admired."

Bobcat said, "Fair enough," and took the lovely belt Coyote had made and already shown to all of his friends.

"All right," said Bobcat, "now here is the song." Bobcat sang thus:

Blind is he who follows me

The brush is dark

Weak is she who follows me

The Mountain is steep

The air holds me

The air holds me

The air holds me

It covers me darting away

Coyote learned the song. "Oh, I can tell this song is powerful," he said with excitement. "Thank you, Bobcat."

Coyote then went home. He thought of resting and starting the song the next night. But he was even more excited still when he was alone in his house. He took each of the special objects out of the leather sack and set them in a circle around his table—the obsidian chunk, the square of oak bark, the tawny ball of clay, and the many, many other special objects he was given. He thought of setting the objects on the chairs at his table, then thought better of it. "What difference does it make?" he said to himself. "There is a large circle of objects—the room will be full." He sang the shape-shifting song, and it became clear that he never had any notion to make belts.

"Old Man Crow," he said out loud.

"Elk," he said out loud.

"Bobcat," he said out loud then.

And on and on. He went from object to object calling out a villager's name, one after the other. At long last his house was full of people, each an exact double of every person in the village. He had all the people he wanted to talk with—and what a chorus of conversations.

Coyote worried that someone passing his house might hear the many people talking and then knock on his door. He worried too about what he would do with the people when morning came. He figured he would keep them locked in his house until he thought of a plan to take care of them. But that is not what happened. With all of the lively conversation, Coyote grew tired and soon fell asleep. When he woke, not a single person was in the house: Coyote found himself looking at his open front door, morning light spilling through. There was not a soul around. When Coyote fell asleep, the new people quickly grew lonesome without him. They missed visiting and talking with him. They gathered near the leather sack by the door, where they had been kept as objects just hours before. Coyote knew what had happened: They saw the door and went out. He remembered what Bobcat had said about the transformed objects retaining something of Coyote's character. Like Coyote, the new people went looking for someone to visit. They would need more and more people to talk with. They had wandered off, spread themselves throughout the village.

Alas, they attached themselves each and every one to their double, the new Old Man Crow to the old Old Man Crow, new Elk to old Elk, seven new Bat Brothers to the seven old Bat Brothers. The original people panicked. They were frightened at seeing these identical beings standing at their sides—frightened, for these new beings said nothing, only stood there waiting for their twins to talk.

"What has happened?" the original people wondered. "This is terrible. These new people that look like us seem like ghosts. They want to be with us, but they don't talk. They just stand looking at us. What do they want? What are they expecting us to do?"

The original people tried to get away from their doubles, but the ghostlike twins followed, keeping pace even as the original people began to run from them.

Quail screamed, "A curse has come upon us!"

Others began to scream also. "Flee, flee!" the first people hollered.

"But how?" cried Quail.

"Like this," said Bobcat, who was singing his shape-shifting song:

> *Blind is he who follows me*
>
> *The brush is dark*
>
> *Weak is she who follows me*
>
> *The Mountain is steep*
>
> *The air holds me*
>
> *The air holds me*
>
> *The air holds me*
>
> *It covers me darting away*

He was singing for all of the villagers, calling out each of their names. And, one by one, the original people were transformed. Quail grew pretty gray feathers, Eagle grew powerful wings, Bear grew fearsome claws—all of them were transformed in that way as they streamed after Bobcat and fled the village.

Coyote watched from his front door. Then he went to the center of the village. There were the new people, lost without their twins, collected around Coyote. Desperate for his company, they pressed close, so close that they began to smother him.

Chicken Hawk, hunting on the far side of the Mountain, had heard the villagers screaming. By the time he returned to the village, he found his pitiful uncle mobbed by these new beings and gasping for air.

"Help me, Nephew! Please help me!" cried Coyote.

"You've done a foolish thing, Uncle," said Chicken Hawk. "Look what has happened."

"I know, I know," gasped Coyote, struggling for air. "But, please—can't you find a way to send these odd people away and bring back the villagers?"

"Look what has happened," Chicken Hawk repeated.

Coyote happened to blink and, when he opened his eyes, he saw that his nephew too had changed form. He was now a striking hunting bird with black and gray markings perched atop an oak tree.

"Oh, not you too," lamented Coyote. "You are going to leave me too."

Coyote began to cry. "Can't we bring the villagers back? Can't we please get rid of these strange people smothering me?"

Chicken Hawk made a sharp whistling sound—the sound he makes in the sky to this day—and the new people stepped back from Coyote so that he could breathe.

"Now listen to me, Uncle," Chicken Hawk said. "The world

is forever fixed now. Don't you see what you have done?"

"I just wanted friends. What was wrong with that? I was lonesome."

"Uncle—just as Bobcat and I tried to tell you, there is nothing wrong with having friends. I tried to warn you. Bobcat too told you to think about what you were going to do..."

"But..."

"No buts about it, Uncle. Why wasn't it enough to sit amongst your friends, making a belt for them—doing something nice for them? You were thinking of yourself again, Uncle. Think about it. At the very least you could have asked them about *their* work, you could have asked them about *their* lives. But all you wanted was for them to talk about *your* belt, what *you* were doing. You were selfish. Remember, if you want a good friend, you must be a good friend."

These last words stung Coyote. He remembered his pride over the beautiful belt; he saw himself showing off to his friends, and he was ashamed beyond measure. He had not listened to Bobcat's warning to think about what he was doing and who he was doing it for.

"Am I ever going to learn?" Coyote repeated again and again to himself. "I just keep making mistakes."

"I believe you will learn," said Chicken Hawk. "The world is fixed anew. The consequences of your selfishness will stare you in the face now—not just when you see your lovely wife looking up at the sons you threw into the sky, but everywhere, everywhere you look."

Chicken Hawk gestured with his wing to the open sky above him. There Coyote saw Eagle flying ever so high. Coyote saw Quail Woman scratching amidst a pile of leaves, and Old Man Crow preening his black feathers on a bay laurel branch, and Elk, further off, grazing on clover.

"Yes," said Coyote sadly, "I will see what I have done and every day feel like hiding, like crawling into a hole."

"Oh, come now," said Chicken Hawk. "You have work to do. Now you must lead the people."

"Lead the people? A pitiful fool like me?"

"Yes, you, Uncle. You are more fit than ever to be a leader. You know to be a good friend to all of the villagers first and foremost—and everywhere you look you will be reminded to think of others in everything you do, any decisions you make."

"Well, I learned to be a good husband the hard way."

"And a better leader, I might add. And now an even better leader."

"But who am I going to lead? These strange beings I created?"

"No, Uncle, you will join the other original beings from the village out in the brush. But first you must send these new people away. You must fix them so they don't follow you."

"How am I going to do that?"

"They are waiting for someone to talk to. Don't forget, they are like you were when you made them—they are lonesome and they have forgotten the stories. They don't know how to live; they don't know who they are. They are waiting to hear the stories. That is what they want. Tell them the stories, and then they will be content and not feel lonesome."

And, right then, Coyote did as his wise nephew Chicken Hawk suggested. He told all of the stories, about Centipede's footrace, about Lizard abducting Rock's daughters, and about Mole and his two wives. At long last, he was done talking, and the new people were happy. They looked around and saw the animals and plants and, at the same time, knew the stories of all these wondrous things. But still they did not leave the village.

"Now how do I get them to leave?" Coyote asked Chicken Hawk.

"Bobcat, before he left the village, threw that beautiful belt you traded him into the sky. The white clamshell disc beads became the white ring you will see at times around the moon. The abalone pendants became the rays on your other son as he climbs the top of this Mountain each morning. Don't despair; your sons have gifts from you now, beautiful necklaces. As for the leather sack, it fell to the earth. Look yonder to the western end of the village."

Coyote looked and found a road there.

"The strip of leather that you used for the belt has become the road that leads down the Mountain and goes on forever. Take the new people to the road. They will follow it with all of the stories in their heads and, that way, create human villages all over the earth."

Coyote took the people to the road. He wished them well.

Then he went back to the center of the village, where he found himself alone. Chicken Hawk was still perched atop the oak tree, and Coyote said, "Now what am I supposed to do?"

"Join the rest of us," answered Chicken Hawk.

"But how, Nephew?"

"Have you looked at yourself, Uncle?"

Coyote smarted: He had four legs and a bushy tail.

"Don't worry, Uncle," said Chicken Hawk. "Now you can be with your villagers again—and of course with your lovely wife."

Coyote forgot about his new four-legged form, thinking only of the joy of joining his lovely wife and the villagers again. He started off for the brush. But as he passed one of the houses, he noticed that one of the new people hadn't left the village with the others. The man was standing looking up at the sun.

As you might guess, that man was Coyote's double. He became the ancestor of all the humans who populated the village there near the top of Sonoma Mountain, that same ancient village from the time when the plants and animals were still people. They say that man married a woman from Cotati. Was that woman Frog Woman's double?

Sometimes, still, Coyote returns to the old village, mostly at night. He hides behind a tree or clump of brush and watches the new people. He sees them sitting by their fires telling stories. Sometimes, they gaze up at the moon, enraptured by its glow. In spring the sound of frogs from the nearby pond charms them. Coyote is happy then. He knows the world is right and the people are home. Occasionally, unable to help himself, he will howl or yelp with joy; but before the people give him too much attention, he goes off again.

Part 16

*T*he day was beautiful, warm. The twin sisters, Question Woman and Answer Woman, continued sitting atop the fence rail on Gravity Hill. It was spring. Birds sang. Cows in the distance grazed. Sonoma Mountain was awash in spectacular color.

"I am thinking of so many things after hearing about how Coyote created people," said Question Woman. "And I'm confused. Are you and I people or are we crows?"

"We are all people still," answered Answer Woman. "Some of us took the form of animals, some the form of human beings. But the point is, we are all relatives. We are all related. We have eyes and ears. We all talk. We all have stories. We come from the same village, after all. That is the lesson of this Mountain."

"But people can't hear us. I mean they hear us, but they don't know what we are saying. That man who just rode by on his bicycle, he might hear us squawk, but he doesn't know what we are saying."

"The Old People of the village, the human descendants of Coyote, they could understand the animals. They communicated with the animals and plants through songs and dreams—and of course through the stories. You see, in the stories we are always both humans and animals. That is, we are all People. But the newest people, the people who left this Mountain and then came back, many of them are called the Forgetters, the humans who forgot the stories of this Mountain."

"What happened?"

"They went away, settled in places all over the world with the stories that they could use for wherever they settled. They could change the stories to suit the places they settled as long as the stories taught them the same lessons, that we are all one People—animals, plants, and human beings—and that we must always think of and remember one another that way."

"Oh, yes, that makes me think of what you said a while back, before the last story. I asked where the cows and starlings came from..."

"And the wild turkeys."

"Yes, so it was these Forgetter People who brought them?"

"Yes, Sister. That is right. Many things happened when the Forgetter People returned here. They brought new animals and plants, yes. But the Forgetters also killed all of the bears and the elk and the pronghorn. They cut down trees. You see, they forgot the stories. They forgot we are all one People, and the animals, indeed the entire Mountain, began to suffer. Now we must all try to learn to live together. We must all remember the stories again."

"But how?"

"Well, we must tell the stories and ask that everyone learn from them. People can always change the stories to suit their needs as long as the stories teach the same lessons of love and respect for all of life."

"The stories can change?"

"Of course. I said so already. The stories always change for different times and different places."

"Like what? Give me an example."

"Well, let's take the first story I told you. Do you remember that story?"

"Have you forgotten I am Question Woman? I forget things."

"Oh, yes. Well, it was the story of the pretty woman and the necklace."

"Oh, I do remember now. She wanted a necklace to impress a man in a village at the edge of Cotati Plain."

"Right. See, she was a human being..."

"Yes."

"So let's go back to the beginning of the stories I told you. Let's go back to that first story. We will add to it so that it makes sense and connects to all of the stories I told you."

"How are you going to do that?"

"I am going to tell you a story."

"What story?"

"Listen."

The Pretty
Woman Latches
Her Necklace

*T*here once was a very pretty woman who lived near the top of Sonoma Mountain, in a village alongside the headwaters of Copeland Creek. She fancied a young man from the bottom of the Mountain, who lived in a village at the edge of Cotati Plain. Despite her beauty, this pretty woman felt unsure of herself. She worried that the young man she fancied might find another pretty woman to marry, since he lived at the bottom of the Mountain, where many beautiful women from near and far often visited the village.

"I worry that this man will not find me attractive," the pretty woman told her father.

"But how is that, daughter? You are young and beautiful and come from good people."

Her father was a well-respected man; he possessed many songs, and people throughout the village sought his advice. They say this man was the nephew of the chief. He advised his daughter not to push her luck, that she should stand before the young man on her own merits. He reminded her that pushing one's luck, much like trickery, often brought regret. Most importantly, he reminded her that true beauty, beauty that is everlasting, comes from the heart. "Such beauty," he said to her, "is stronger and more appealing than any beauty that might first meet the eyes. This young man you wish to marry, if he is worthy, will value beauty that is true and everlasting."

This wise father gave his pretty daughter a beautiful necklace in order that the young man—indeed all of the people in the young man's village—would know who she was and where she came from.

"Do you even know yet if this young man is worthy of you?" asked her father. "If indeed he is a worthy man and happens to overlook you, this necklace will make him take notice of you."

"But will the necklace force him to marry me? Will the necklace charm him?"

"You don't want to force anyone to marry you," said her father. "You don't want to charm or trick a man. The young man must be someone who appreciates your true beauty."

Unfortunately, this very pretty woman did not take her father's advice. She had a dream of a hillside—she actually knew of the hill, which wasn't too far from her village—and she saw a string of rocks just below the hill's crest. She woke and, charmed by what she saw in her dream, figured she would make a necklace with those rocks that would be far more beautiful than the necklace her father had given her. That way she would certainly capture the young man's heart. She employed the help of many animals in order to carry the rocks and then grind them down to size. But, in the end, her pile of grounddown rocks washed down Copeland Creek, spilling near the bottom of the Mountain, just below the bridge on Lichau Road. The pretty woman chased down the mountainside after her rocks. She looked for those rocks, walking along the creek bed, but could not find them. It was a silly dream and a silly idea. Her father tried to reason with her, but she would not quit searching for those rocks.

Many years passed, and the father became more and more worried about his daughter.

"I miss my daughter. How can I help her?" he wondered aloud.

This wise father knew many good things; but on the matter of a young woman's love for a man, he thought he should consult the Council of Wise Women Governors. These four old women advised even the chief on important matters concerning the villagers and life on the Mountain.

"You did everything right," these old women told the father. "That necklace made of clamshell disc beads and abalone pendants contained the songs and stories of this wondrous Mountain, each bead a song, each pendant a story. If your pretty daughter went to Cotati Village wearing that necklace, the young man she set her heart on, as well as all of the villagers there, would take special note of her, for they would recognize in that necklace all of the songs and stories she carried within her heart from the Mountain. Thus, they would not only find her beautiful to see but also know her true worth."

"Yes," said the sad father, "that is what I told her. I said the young man and the villagers would know that she came from this place where good people with good stories live."

"But did you remind her that she had the stories within her

heart—that the necklace was just a reflection of her true and everlasting beauty?"

"Well, maybe I didn't explain it quite that way," answered the father.

"Find the necklace, then go to the bottom of the Mountain and talk to your daughter," the four Wise Women told him.

"But can I get through to her? Will she listen to me?"

The Wise Women did not hear this last question, for, by the time the father finished talking, the four old women had gone. Many times over the years the father had approached his daughter, pleading with her to return home, but to no avail. She was so obsessed with finding her lost rocks amidst the thousands of other rocks in the creek bed that she often would not even look up and acknowledge that her father was trying to talk to her. She believed still, even after many years, that if she found those rocks and put a necklace together she would be able to attract the young man from Cotati Village.

The wise father had no option but to try to talk to his daughter again, as the four old women suggested. In his daughter's empty bedroom, he found the necklace he had given her, which she had left on the floor, and then he went down to the bottom of the hill. There, just below the bridge over Copeland Creek, he found his pretty daughter walking amidst the rocks. This sight always saddened him greatly, for he could not bear to see his daughter so alone and beside herself. Holding the necklace up, he said, "Daughter, please look up and remember me."

The pretty woman looked up and the glinting abalone pendants caught her attention. A faint memory of the beautiful necklace stirred in her. She stood looking for the longest time, and her father was happy that for the moment she had ceased her endless wandering along the creek bed.

"You wanted a certain young man and I offered you this necklace in order that you might appeal to him," the father said, choosing his words carefully, "but I forgot to remind you of something important."

She looked at her father, yet the poor man was not certain that she recognized him, that she wasn't only interested in how the necklace might help her in her pursuit. At least ten years had passed since this pretty woman left her village. All that time she had been wandering the creek bed day and night, and her father wondered if she still knew who he was.

"Listen, please," the father pleaded. "It is me, your father, and I must tell you that this necklace contains the songs and stories of your home, this wondrous Mountain. Each shell bead contains a song, and each abalone pendant one of the stories. Please, Daughter, take the necklace with you and wear it for the young man and all of his villagers to see, for the necklace is but a mere reflection of these songs and stories in your heart—your true and everlasting beauty."

To her father's surprise, the pretty woman reached out and took the necklace. She even thanked him, calling him Father, which showed that she recognized him. But there was little feeling in her words. The sad father knew as much, and he made his way back up the Mountain.

The pretty woman figured that Cotati Village was not that far away and that, after searching the creek bed for so many years, she might try something new. So she went there. But she did not wear the necklace. Though it glinted in the sunlight and was beautiful, she thought it would do little to add to her beauty. She carried it in her dress pocket, saying to herself, "I might look silly wearing this thing; and, indeed if it has so much power, then the man of my dreams will notice me even if it is in my dress pocket."

The villagers of Cotati welcomed her. They offered her fresh blackberries to eat and were kind, but none seemed particularly impressed. She was treated with the same hospitality offered to any guest. Worse for this pretty woman, she saw the young man she fancied and he paid her little attention. He was busy weaving a basket, and after looking up to see who had come into the village, he went back to his work. The pretty woman was so infuriated that when she got back to the creek bed there below the bridge, she threw the necklace to the ground with such force that it broke into a million tiny pieces, disc beads and pendants scattering everywhere.

Her father then shortly returned to see how her visit to Cotati Village had gone. Once again, to his surprise, she immediately recognized him. But she was angry.

"That necklace was worthless," she scoffed. "I broke it into a million pieces."

When she told her father how she had carried it in her dress pocket, he said, "Well of course you got no special treatment, for the villagers could not see it."

"Why must they see it?" the daughter argued. "I thought you said I was already beautiful enough."

"You are beautiful enough," answered her father. "But you were ashamed of that necklace, and the villagers, if they noticed anything particular about you, it was your shame."

"So what must I do now?" the pretty woman asked with little heart in her voice.

The father, again greatly hurt by his daughter's disregard, wondered if she would listen to anything he had to say. Still, he answered her. "You must find the disc beads and pendants and put the necklace back together again and then show it to the villagers just as I first told you."

The saddened, wise father wanted to say more, but it was clear to him that his pretty daughter was no longer listening. She had turned back to the creek.

Surprisingly, the pretty woman gathered up as many disc beads and pendants as she could find; and then, with them cupped in her hands, she traveled back to Cotati Village. But, alas, the people there were but generous and kind again, as with any guest, and the young man looked up from his basket only once and then went back to his weaving.

Once back at the creek, and even angrier than before, the pretty woman hurled the beads and pendants to the ground. And as before, he father came, curious about her last visit.

"You are trying to deceive me," she accused.

"Daughter, I wanted to tell you before that if the necklace wasn't strung together just as when I gave it to you, it would have no power. You turned your back on me. Now you must listen to me and put the necklace back together—string the beads and pendants—and only then wear it for all to see."

The pretty woman stood looking at her father for some time. When she turned back to the creek once more, he left. He still wasn't convinced that his daughter listened to what he had to say.

She had listened, but only as before, with the desperate hope that she might at last capture the handsome young man's heart. She searched the creek bed and found the many beads and pendants that she had for a second time left scattered on the ground. Then, sitting on a rock near the water, she began to sort the beads and pendants, trying to remember the necklace's pattern. The beautiful beads and glinting pendants intrigued her, and for the first time she forgot about the handsome man. Bead by bead, pendant after pendant, she began to reassemble the necklace as she remembered it. As she sewed, attaching each bead and pendant to the strip of deer hide, a strange and uncomfortable feeling began to come over her. She was lonesome, for now, and as she held each bead and pendant, she remembered yet another song and story of her home, the wondrous Mountain that she had forgotten for so many years. She worked and worked, day and night, for without hearing these songs and stories, she could not bear the loneliness. She was so taken with these memories from her home that when at last she finished the necklace she could do nothing but touch each bead and pendant, singing the songs and telling the stories aloud over and over until each was planted firmly in her heart and singing there.

One morning, before she knelt over the creek to wash her face, she draped the necklace over a pair of small branches. There, glinting in the pool of water, was the reflection of the necklace, the white beads each a speck of light and the abalone pendants a thousand tiny dancing rainbows. There too, moving over the glassy surface of the water amidst the reflections, was her face. Her heart turned and fluttered. She knew the Mountain had always been there for her, and in that reflection she saw how beautiful she was in the specks of light and glinting tiny rainbows of the Mountain's songs and stories.

She straightened and looked then at the necklace draped over the branches. She heard birds singing and, beyond the creek bed, saw the hillsides awash in color, as if for the first time. "I am alive again," she said.

Taking the necklace, she started off, again to Cotati Village. But before she reached the village, before anyone even saw her coming, she remembered that she was still carrying the necklace instead of wearing it as her wise father had instructed. What's more, she remembered that she could not wear the necklace even if she wanted, for despite her careful searching of the creek bed she had been unable to find the necklace's clasp, beautiful and made of abalone shell like the pendants. She was not saddened or worried, however—not as she had been before; for some time she had forgotten about the handsome young man and now didn't feel so desperate to enter his village.

She went home to her village up the Mountain. The sight of the people and the houses flooded her with joy. "Oh, I will never leave again," she vowed to herself.

She went to her father's house and, upon seeing him, felt great trepidation, for she remembered how she had disregarded him, and she felt ashamed. But, being the wise man that he was, he welcomed her warmly, thankful that she was home and safe and happy. She told him about how she strung the necklace anew with the beads and pendants and how then the beautiful songs and stories came back to her.

"But there is one thing missing, Father," she said. "I cannot find the abalone shell clasp and therefore I cannot wear the necklace as you instructed. Of course I would be happy to stay home and not have to go anywhere wearing the necklace if that would be all right."

"Well, I don't know the answer to your concerns," the wise father said, looking at his pretty daughter across the kitchen table. "I know many things, but on these matters I think we should consult the Council of Wise Women Governors."

The wise father and his pretty daughter gathered in a circle inside the four old Wise Women's ceremonial house.

"You have learned your lesson well," said the first old Wise Woman to the pretty woman. "You forgot yourself. Just like every person in the stories, you had something to learn."

Next the second old Wise Woman spoke. "Passion—desire for a man or woman—can be like greed. If there is not true love, you might become so taken with a handsome person that you can think of nothing else. You become selfish, you forget your friends and family, you forget where you come from, and you forget who you are and your true beauty—all in that order."

"Yes, that is what happened to me," said the pretty woman.

Then the third old Wise Woman spoke. "So now you know your story, pretty woman. You too have a story: You forgot yourself over a man."

"Yes, 'The Pretty Woman Who Forgot Herself,'" said the pretty woman.

"Well, there's more," continued the third old Wise Woman.

"Yes?"

"Yes. You have been fixed as a storyteller. You have memorized the songs and stories so that now they are forever singing in your heart. You can now travel the land telling the stories of this wondrous Mountain."

"But, dear kind third Wise Woman, I cannot wear the necklace as I go about, for I have lost its clasp. Yet I would be perfectly happy to stay home and never wander again if that would be all right."

Then the fourth old Wise Woman spoke. "Ah, pretty woman, but you have no choice. As my wise sister just told you: You have been fixed; you must go."

"But what of the missing clasp?"

"That is the point," answered the fourth old Wise Woman.

"You will not be known as 'The Pretty Woman Who Forgot Herself,' no. My goodness, many people forget themselves. Isn't that the lesson of so many stories?"

"True," answered the pretty woman. "So who will I be? What will be my story?"

The fourth old Wise Woman pointed to the beautiful necklace in the pretty woman's hands. "The last pendant there represents your story. Your story will be called 'The Pretty Woman Latches Her Necklace.' The stories must be connected after all, and you must connect your story to the others—you must connect your pendant to the other pendants. You must latch the necklace."

"But how?" said the pretty woman. "I have lost the necklace's clasp!"

"You know how," answered the fourth old Wise Woman.

They all sat quietly while the pretty woman thought about what this last old Wise Woman said. The wise father, proud of his pretty daughter, anxiously awaited her response. Then, without saying a word beforehand, the pretty woman began singing:

Seeing Forever

My eyes, my eyes

I offer you

Seeing Truth

My eyes, my eyes

I offer you

Seeing Lies

My eyes, my eyes

I offer you

Seeing Forever

This song, this song

I sing for you

Over and over the pretty woman chanted. It was the Eagle's song.

"Yes," said the fourth old Wise Woman. "With that song you will have the eyes of the Eagle and easily will find the clasp."

The four old Wise Women then spoke in unison. "You have found in the stories an answer. You have made the connection with the song that you needed. For that is the final lesson, to look and see how your story can be connected to all of the other stories. That way the stories can help you."

"I see that now," said the pretty woman. "All of the answers I need in my life are in the stories."

"Yes, exactly. That is the lesson," answered the four old Wise Women. "Think about the stories and they will think about you. Forget about the stories and they will forget about you."

"Oh, I understand," said the pretty woman.

After thanking the four old Wise Women for their good counsel, the pretty woman and her father got up to leave.

"Not so fast," said the fourth old Wise Woman, "not so fast. After you find the clasp for the necklace and clasp the necklace around your neck, you will have a special song to sing as you travel about. That way, people will hear you coming and know it is time for stories. Their minds will fill with wonder. And what is wonder but hunger for a story? Listen," said the fourth old Wise Woman, and she began singing:

Singing, talking

A band of charms

Turning to stories

Turning to light

Turning to light

Turning to light

This band of stones

The light in your heart

After hearing the song, the pretty woman and her wise father again thanked the four old Wise Women for their good counsel.

Then the pretty woman left her village. She was lonely, missing her father and the villagers; but, as she knew so well, her home, this wondrous Mountain, would be in her heart wherever she traveled, however far she journeyed. With the Eagle's song, she found the necklace's abalone clasp. Then she lifted the necklace to her neck and latched the necklace.

She traveled first to Cotati Village. As she approached the village, she was singing:

> *Singing, talking*
>
> *A band of charms*
>
> *Turning to stories*
>
> *Turning to light*
>
> *Turning to light*
>
> *Turning to light*
>
> *This band of stones*
>
> *The light in your heart*

The villagers congregated to hear her stories, crowded close to her until the wee hours of the morning. At daylight, she started north toward Santa Rosa, to the next village. Halfway there, near a bend in the road, she felt someone following her. When she turned to see who was there, she found a stranger. She did not recognize the white teeth and shiny hair; rather her gaze was fixed on the basket in the person's hands. The basket's intricate design of crisscrossing patterns intrigued her, and she could not stop looking at it. She thought it was the most beautiful basket she had ever seen. When she looked up and saw the person holding the basket, she knew he was no stranger.

"I began weaving this basket with no idea why," the handsome young man said to her.

Seeing him, she barely remembered the young man she had fancied for so long. Certainly he was the same man, handsome and strong, but he was beautiful to her in a way she had never imagined. Her heart beat fast, a million melodies inside of her ringing all at the same time.

"I listened to your songs and stories all night," he said. "And then I knew why I made the basket. Wasn't my heart speaking to me all along? The basket's design matches your songs and stories. It is the design of the earth, and your songs and stories match the earth's design. You will go all over the earth telling stories. You can put the necklace in the basket."

"But I am to wear the necklace on my neck," she told him.

"Ah, yes, but the basket can let people know you are approaching."

"But my song does that," she said.

"You will go far. The earth will get noisy and crowded in the future. The Forgetters will come, the ones who forget the stories. People might not be able to hear you singing them. Please, give me the necklace and let me show you something."

The pretty woman hesitated, but, hearing the words of the four old Wise Women in what the young man said about her traveling here and there to tell stories, she acquiesced and handed him her necklace.

He took the necklace and draped it over the top of the basket. Then he walked to the top of a nearby hill and set down the basket and necklace. When he returned, she was perplexed.

"What are you doing?" she asked him.

He pointed to the top of the hill. Clouds pitched and rolled there. She saw nothing else. But then when the sun flashed between the clouds, to her amazement an enormous rainbow rose from the basket high into the sky.

"You see," the handsome young man said, "everywhere you go now you will have a rainbow to let people know where you are. Even the Forgetters, they will see the rainbow and wonder and then be hungry for a story."

"But how did you make the rainbow?" the pretty woman asked, still perplexed.

"I wove the basket tight enough to hold water. The basket holds a little pool of water from Copeland Creek. It is enough water, all that is needed to reflect into the sky a necklace so beautiful."

That's what happened then. The last magic spirit on the Mountain was created: the Rainbow. The handsome young man, following the long established tradition, asked ever so humbly if the pretty woman would teach him a special song that he could learn in order to become her true and loving husband. As you might guess, she taught him the song he first heard her singing when she approached the village. And now that they are married, the two of them go about singing the song as he accompanies her to tell the stories. The two voices are quite loud. But if the world is too noisy, anyone can still see a rainbow.

The pretty woman often returned home to visit her father and the other villagers. But then she was on her way again, joining her husband at Cotati Village. People claim that you can sometimes still see the pretty woman coming and going. They say the best place to catch a glimpse of her is just past the bridge over Copeland Creek. She's often sitting amidst the rocks, perhaps remembering her story. Maybe it's her daughter or granddaughter, or maybe her spirit. People say they have heard her singing her beautiful song even when they have not been able to spot her. One man claims that while hiking amidst the rocks there early one morning he found her sitting on a rock behind a clump of willow. He heard her telling stories. She started, he said, by saying to him, "This is the story of Sonoma Mountain."

About the Author

Greg Sarris is currently serving his thirteenth term as Chairman of the Federated Indians of Graton Rancheria. He holds the Graton Rancheria Endowed Chair in Writing and Native American Studies at Sonoma State University, and his publications include *Keeping Slug Woman Alive: A Holistic Approach to American Indian Texts* (1993), *Grand Avenue* (1994), and *Watermelon Nights* (1999). Greg lives and works in Sonoma County. Visit his website at www.greg-sarris.com.

Discussion Guide for *How a Mountain Was Made*

1. Greg Sarris has described *How a Mountain Was Made* as a story cycle, a collection of stories revolving around a main narrative theme. How does this idea of a story cycle affect your understanding of each individual story, and of the story collection as a whole?

2. While being deeply inspired by Coast Miwok and Southern Pomo creation stories, this book is an authored work from the twenty-first century. What can literature do or convey that oral tradition cannot, and vice versa?

3. How does the geographic specificity of Sonoma Mountain affect the moral code of *How a Mountain Was Made*? Are the morals of these stories universal, context-dependent, or somewhere in between?

4. "Coyote Creates a Costume Fit for a Chief," "Coyote Throws His Sons into the Sky," and other stories examine the meaning of good leadership. How does Coyote's relationship to leadership change throughout the course of *How a Mountain Was Made*?

5. How does song function in this written, or perhaps spoken, communication form? Why does Sarris include the lyrics of songs?

6. If you reread "The Pretty Woman and the Necklace," what nuances do you notice that can come only from reading the rest of the book? How does the order of information dictate or challenge the power relationship among stories?

7. Even though much of *How a Mountain Was Made* takes place in a time "when all the animals were still people," the characters often have the physical traits and characteristics of mammals, birds, insects, and even natural phenomena. What does this say about what it means to be a part of (or excluded from) a community? Does this extend to non-humans? Non-biological things?

Printed in the USA
CPSIA information can be obtained
at www.ICGtesting.com
CBHW061810030524
7761CB00007B/22